ᑭᕕᐅᑉ ᐊᐅᓪᓛᓂᖕᒐ
Kiviuq's Journey

ᐅᓂᑉᑳᖅᑕᐅᒃᑲᓐᓂᖅᑐᖅ • Retold by

ᕼᐃᓐᕆ ᐃᖢᐊᖅᓂᖅ
Henry Isluanik

ᑎᑎᕋᐅᔭᖅᑕᐅᔪᖅ • Illustrated by

ᔾᕐᒪᐃᓐ ᐊᕐᓇᑦᑕᐅᔪᖅ
Germaine Arnaktauyok

ᐱᒋᐊᕐᓂᖕᖕᒦ • Preface

ᑲᐅᔭᓚᑦᑕᐅᖅᑕᐃ ᕼᐊᖕᕆ ᐃᓗᐊᕐᓂᖅ ᖃᖕᖕᓚᕐᔪᐊᖅ ᐊᕐᕕᐊᓄᑦᐊᖅᖕᒪᑎᓇᓪᒧᖕᓗ. ᐱᓴᕆᖕᖕᔫᑕᐅᖅᕐᒥᓪᒪᒪ ᖃᐅᔨᓴᐃᐊᖅᖕᒪ ᐅᓂᐸᖅᑐᐊᖅᑐᖕᓂᖕ ᐊᐱᖅᓱᑎᐊᖅᖅᖕᓗᖕᓗ ᐃᕐᖄᕐᓂᖅ ᑭᐊᕐᓯᕐᒥ ᓄᓇᕗᑦᒥ. ᒪᑯᓯ ᑲᓗᐊᖅ ᐅᖅᑲᐅᑎᒪᓕᕈᑦ ᐊᐱᖅᓱᖅᖕᑲᕐᖕᐅᓂᖕ ᐊᖕᐅᒐᓂ ᐃᓗᐊᕐᓂᖅ. ᐃᓗᐊᕐᓂᖅ ᖃᕿ ᓄᒪᐅᕐᕿᐃᖅᖕᒪᕐᖕ ᒪᑯᕈᕿ ᐃᑭᕐᕿᐊᑕᐅᖅᕐᖕᒪ ᐅᖅᖅᖕᑎᐅᕿᓗ ᐅᓂᐸᖅᑐᑎᕐᔫ. ᑕᒪᓪ ᓯᓪᓗᐊᖕᖕᑕᑎᐊᖅᕐᖕᑐᒥᖕ ᐅᖅᓪᑐᖅᑭᐸᓚᑕᐅᖅᖅᖕᕐᖕᓚ ᒪᑯᕈᒥᓪᒪ ᐃᓗᐊᕐᓂᕐᒥᓪᓗ, ᑐᖕᓚᐅᕐᑲᖕᓗᖕᕐᖕ ᐊᕐᖅᑲᖕᐸᒃᖅᖕᑲᑎᕐᖕᓗᖕᕐᖕ ᐃᓄᐃᑦ ᐅᓂᐸᖅᑐᑐᖅᖕᕆᕐᓂᖅ ᐊᐱᖅᖅᑎᒪᓕᒥᓪᖕᓗ ᑭᓯᑕᒋᖅᖕᓚᕐᖕᓗᖕᕐᖕ. ᓇᖕᓗᑕᐅᖕᓚ ᖃᐅᔨᓂᖕᕆᕐᓂᖕᕐᖕ ᐅᓂᐸᖅᑐᑐᐊᖅᕐᖅᖕᕐᖕ ᐊᕐᖕᓗ ᖃᓄᐃᑎᐅᕐᓂᖕᓗᖕᐅᖕᐊᕐᖕᐊᖕᕐᖕ ᐃᖅᖅᑕᐅᓪᖅᑎᐊᕐᑕᐅᖕᓚᖕᕐᖕ, ᐊᒻᓚ ᐃᖕᓴᖕᕐᑎᖅᑎᐊᖅᖕᕐᖕᓂᖕᕐᖕ ᐊᕐᖕᓂᖅᖕᑲᖕᓂᖅᖕᑲᑕᐅᖅᕐᖕᓚᖕᕐᖕ ᖃᐅᔨᓚᖕᔒᕐᖕᓂᖕᕐᖕ.

ᐅᑭᐅᓂᖕᕐᖕ ᐊᒦᓇᖕᕐᖕ ᐅᑎᖅᑕᖅᑕᕐᑕᐅᖅᕐᖕᓚ

I met Henry Isluanik many years ago during a trip to Arviat. I was researching traditional stories and interviewing elders in the Kivalliq Region of Nunavut. Mark Kalluak suggested that I interview his older brother, Henry. Henry did not speak English, so Mark offered to help translate during the interview. I ended up spending a very enjoyable afternoon with Mark and Henry, listening as they shared traditional Inuit stories and answered my questions. I was very impressed with their knowledge of traditional stories and lore, their keen memories for details, and how generously they shared their knowledge.

Over the next few years, I travelled back to Arviat several times, and each time I learned more about Inuit traditional stories,

ᑭᕕᐅᑉ
ᐊᐅᑦᑖᓂᕐᒪ

Kiviuq's
Journey

Published in Canada by Inhabit Media Inc. (www.inhabitmedia.com) • Inhabit Media Inc.
(Iqaluit Office), P.O. Box 11125, Iqaluit, Nunavut, X0A 1H0 • (Toronto Office), 146A Orchard View Blvd., Toronto, Ontario, M4R 1C3

Edited by Neil Christopher and Louise Flaherty • Translated by Pelagie Owlijoot • Retold by Henry Isluanik • Illustrated by Germaine Arnaktauyok
Design and layout copyright © 2014 Inhabit Media Inc. • Text copyright © 2014 by Henry Isluanik • Illustrations copyright © 2014 by Inhabit Media Inc.

Printed and bound in Canada

ISBN 978-1-927095-80-5

We acknowledge the support of the Canada Council for the Arts for our publishing program.

We acknowledge the support of the Government of Canada through the Department of Canadian Heritage Canada Book Fund program.

Library and Archives Canada Cataloguing in Publication

Isluanik, Henry, 1925-2012, author
    Kiviup aullaaninga / unipkaaqtaukkanniqtuq Hinri I½uarniq
; titiraujaqtaujuq Jirmain Arnattaujuq = Kiviuq's journey / retold
by Henry Isluanik ; illustrated by Germaine Arnaktauyok.

Summary: Henry Isluanik retells the Kiviuq legend, a version passed
    on to him by his mother, of a courageous hunter who was swept
    out to sea during a storm and who spent many years trying to find
    his way back home.
Text in Inuktitut and English (in syllabic characters). Title in
    Inuktitut romanized.
ISBN 978-1-927095-80-5 (pbk.)

    1. Kiviuq (Legendary character). 2. Inuit--Nunavut--Folklore.
3. Hunters--Nunavut--Folklore. 4. Hunting--Nunavut--Folklore.
5. Courage--Folklore. 6. Folklore--Nunavut. 7. Legends--Nunavut.
I. Arnaktauyok, Germaine, illustrator II. Isluanik, Henry, 1925-2012.
Kiviup aullaaninga. English. III. Title. IV. Title: Kiviuq's journey.

E99.E7I85 2014   398.209719'58   C2014-901395-7

Canadian Heritage   Patrimoine canadien   Canada   Canada Council for the Arts   Conseil des Arts du Canada

Nunavut

ᐊᕐᖀᐊᖕᒧᑦ ᐊᒃᓯᐊᖅᓱᖖᒍᖔᒪ, ᑕᐃᑯᐊᖕᖕᑳᖕᖃᒪᒪ
ᐃᓇᑉᐱᑕᐸᓂᖃᖅᑕᐅᒐᒪ ᐃᓄᐃᑦ
ᐅᓂᖃᑐᐊᑐᖃᖅᒪᓂᓴᓂᒃ, ᖅᕿᔭᓐᓂᖅᐸᒃ
ᒫᑯᔫᓗ ᐃᓄᐊᑦᓂᓯᓗ ᐊᒻᒪ ᐊᖕᖀᐃᑦ ᐊᔨᖓᑦ
ᐅᓂᖃᖅᑕᐅᖃᖅᑐᑦ ᐅᕐᖁᓄᑦ.
ᐱᖕᖀᖃᖅᑎᑕᐅᑎᒃᕋᖃᖅᑕᐅᒐᒪ
ᖃᐅᔨᒪᖃᓂᔫᑦᑐᐊᑐᖅᓱᑎᓄᓗ
ᐱᑕᓂᖃᑎᑎᒃᖅᑐᑦ ᐊᒡᔪᑦ
ᐅᓂᖃᖅᑐᐊᖃᖕᑎᑦ. ᖅᕿᑦᓐᑎᓐᑲᖅᐸᒃ
ᐃᓄᐃᑦ ᐊᒡᔪᑦ ᐊᒡᖃᖕᖃᑎᖃᖅᖃᖅᑕᐅᖅᑐᑦ
ᖅᑲᐅᔨᒪᕐᔾᒣᓂᒃ. ᒫᑯᔫᓗ ᐃᓇᑕᑐᖕᓯᓗ
ᓱᐳᖕᑕᐅᖅᖃᑕᐅᕝ ᖅᕿᓐᓂᖅᖕᐸᔾᑦᓂᓂ ᐃᓄᖕᓂ.
ᐃᑎᔾᒧᔾᓕᒡᒥᖅ ᖅᕿᓐᖁᖕᑲᖅ ᑕᑯᐊᖔ ᐊᖕᐅᔾᑦᖕ.
ᒫᑯᔾ ᑲᓄᖅᓇᑕᐅᖅ ᐃᓄᖅᖔᓇᐃᑕᐅᖅᖅᑐᖅ 2011-
ᒥ. ᒫᑯᔾᓗ ᐱᑕᓇᑕᐅᖅᐳᒃᖔᐸ ᐱᓇᑦᔾᓇᓐᖃᓂᖕᓂ
ᐅᓂᖃᖅᑐᐊᑐᖅᖕᓂᒃ ᐅᖃᖃᓕᑐᐅᖅᖕᓄᑦ.
ᑐᖕᓇᑎᑖᒪᒪ ᐃᓄᔾᖔᖃᐃᐊᖕᓯᖃᖕᖀᓂᒃ
ᐃᑎᒪᖕᑕᐅᖅᐳᖕᒪ, ᓄᖃᖔᖔ ᐊᑎᐅᑝᖃᖅ
ᐊᑕᖔᑐᔾᖔᑎᒡᒥᖅ ᐊᖕᔾᒥᒡᒥᖅ, ᐱᖔᑎᓇᖕᑎᔾᖅ,
ᐃᖁᖕᑎᐊᖕ ᐊᒻᒪ ᖅᑲᐅᔨᒪᖕᔾᖕᖔᖅ ᓯᓴᑐᔾᖅ.
ᐅᑭᐅᑦ ᐊᒡᔾᖕᖕᓇᑎᒡᑐᑦ ᖅᕿᖔᖕᖃᑎᖕᓗᖕᑦ
ᑐᖕᓕᓇᒡᖅᖔᒪ ᐃᓄᑦᖔᓂᖅ ᐃᖁᖕᑲᐃᖔᖔᖃᓐᑎᒡᑐ

thanks to Mark, Henry, and the other community
elders who shared their time with me.

I have been fortunate in my life to have
met and worked with many great storytellers.
I am grateful to many people for sharing their
knowledge with me. And Mark Kalluak and
Henry Isluanik are at the top of my list of
people I must thank. I am deeply grateful to
these two brothers. Mark Kalluak passed away
in 2011. Mark and I were working together
on his third collection of traditional stories at
the time. When I received the news of Mark's
passing, I knew Nunavut had lost a brilliant
man. Mark was so humble and kind, and filled
with so much knowledge. Then, a year later, I
heard the news of Henry's passing.

Although Henry and I talked
many times, unfortunately, we never had
an opportunity to work on a book together.
As I was reviewing videotaped interviews
from Arviat, I found Henry's version of the

ᐅᖅᑲᖅᑎᒌᕚᑕᐅᕋᔪᐊᖅᐅᓐᓗᑎᖅ ᐃᑐᐊᕐᓂᕐᓗ
ᐅᒃᔪᐊᖅᐳᖕᒐ ᐅᖅᑲᓕᑕᐅᕐᓯᒪᖓᓂᐊᓪᓂᖅ.
ᑕᑑᕐᖅᑎᓐᒍᓪᒐ ᓂᐱᑎᐅᓂᑯᕐᑎᓂᖅ
ᐊᕐᐊᕐᒥᐅᓂᖅ ᓇᓇᑕᐅᖅᐸᑦ
ᐃᒍᐊᕐᓂᐅᑦ ᐅᓂᐸᖅᑐᐊᕐᒥ. ᐃᒍᐊᕐᓂᐅᑦ
ᐅᖅᑲᐅᑎᑕᐅᕐᒪᕐᒥ ᐅᒃᔪᐊᕐᓂᕐᕐᑐᓂ
ᐊᒥᒃᔭᐊᑦ ᓴᖅᑭᑕᐅᕐᒫᑎᓐᓗᑦ ᐅᖅᑲᓕᒪᐃ
ᐊᒻᒪ ᑕᓇᓕᖕᑦ ᐅᓂᐸᖅᑎᒪᕐᒥᒐᒥ
ᐊᑕᕐᑦᑎᐊᑐᖕᒐ ᐅᓂᐸᖅᑐᐊᕐᒥ.
ᐅᖅᑲᐅᑎᑕᐅᕐᒪᕐᒥ ᐅᓂᐸᑐᐊᕐᓂᕐᑐᓂ
ᐊᑕᕐᑎᓐᑎᐊᑐᖕᒐ ᓯᒋᕐᑎᓂᓗ.
ᐱᒪᓇᐅᑎᑕᐅᕐᒪᐅ ᑐᒃᑐᓗᕆᓂ ᐅᓂᐸᖅᑐᐊᕐᒥ
ᓴᖅᑭᑕᐅᕐᑯᒋᓗ. ᐃᑲᕐᒃᑎᓐᕐᓗ ᐱᓕᐃ
ᐊᐳᑕᐸᕐᑎ ᐊᐱᓂᑕᐅᕐᒃᐸᕐᑦ ᐃᒍᐊᕐᓂᐅᑦ
ᐃᑕᒥᐸᕐᑎ ᐋᒻᒪᖕᕐᒐᑕ
ᓴᖅᑎᓐᑎᕐᒐᑕᐅᕐᒃᑕ
ᐅᓂᐸᕐᓂᓇᐅᓗᓂᖅ ᑭᐅᐅᒋᕐᖅ. ᐋᒻᒪᖕᑕᐅᕐᒪᕐᑕ
ᑕᐅᓪ ᓴᖅᑎᓐᑕᐅᕐᔭᐅᓇᖅᑭᑴᖅ. ᐃᒍᐊᕐᓂᕐᖅ
ᕐᑯᐊᐊᕐᔪᓕᖕᒐᑕᐅᕐᒪᕐᑦ ᖅᑲᐳᑕᕐᖅᒥ
ᐅᓂᐸᖅᑐᐊᕐᒪᕐ ᑭᐅᐅᕐᖅ
ᐊᒥᕐᒃᑲᖅᑕᐅᕐᔭᐅᓇᖅᑭᔭᕐᒪᕐᑦ
ᒪᒃᑯᒍᑐᓂᕐᑦ.

ᓂᕐᑦ ᑯᓂᕐᑦᑕᐅᕐ • Neil Christopher

Kiviuq legend. Henry had told me that he was
disappointed at how several books and films
have merged the various versions of this great
story together. He wanted to tell me the version
he had been told in its entirety, as well as the
song that went with it. It was important to him
that the traditional version from his region be
preserved in its original form. With the help of
Pelagie Owlijoot, I approached Henry's family
and asked permission to publish a book based
on his retelling of the legend of Kiviuq. They
kindly agreed, and now we have the book you
are holding. I think Henry would have been
happy to know that his version of the Kiviuq
legend is being shared with a new generation.

ᓯᐅᑦᑕᖅ • Part One

ᐱᒋᐊᕐᓂᐊ • The Beginning

ᑭᐅᐅᑉᖅ ᑕᒪᐅᓐᕐᕈ ᑎᓐᐅᓚᖻᒍᖅ ᕐᓈᓂ ᑐᐱᑦ ᖃᐸᐱᕿᑲᑊᐸᖅ
ᓐᑭᕈᓚᕐᑭᓈᖀᒍᒪᑲᒍᖅ ᐅᕝᓚᓄᑦᗙ ᑕᒪᖁᒪᖅᖢᖅ ᑎᓐᐅᐸᑦ ᓂᖅᕐᑕᐃᓄᑦ
ᓂᖅᑉᖃᓂᖅ ᑲᓐᖅᓯᕐᐊᕈᑦ. ᑕᓐᐅᒰᕐᕐᑎᖅᖃᖅᗒᓐ ᐊᑕᐅᖅ ᐊᖁᓈᖅᖃᓂᖅ
ᐅᖅᕐᑎᖅᖃᓄᖢᗙ ᐅᑭᐅᒍᑦ ᓂᖅᑉᖃᓂᖅ.

ᑕᓐᐅᖅᒳᒪᒍᖅ ᐅᐱᖔᑲᖅᑯᑦ, ᑕᖅᖃᐊᐅᒍᖅ ᐊᖃᓇᑉᗙᐱᑊ
ᒪᒡᐲᖁᒪᗙᒍᖢᓂᖅ ᐃᓕᐊᕐᓚᖢᓂᖅ ᑕᒪᖁᒍᖅ ᐊᖃᓇᑉᗙᐊᖅᗙᖅ
ᐊᕐᖁᔪᐊᖅᖃᒍᒪᖅᗒᓂ ᑐᐱᖕᒥᓂᐊᖁᖢᔪᖅ ᓴᓂᕤᕐᐃᑐᖅᕐᗙᓂ.

Kiviuq was a man who had special powers. He was well known amongst Inuit in different regions because he was a talented, prosperous man. He was always helping the less fortunate and got along well with everyone. He was a good man.

It was springtime. The season when Inuit were camping in the coastal areas because they needed to stock up on sea mammals for the winter. Sea mammals were used for food, as well as to provide oil for their qulliqs (seal-oil lamps).

ᑕᐃᒻᓇᔫᖅ ᐃᙳᑖ ᒪᒃᑯᒃᑐᕐᕋᐊᖅ ᐱᙳᐊᖅᑕᐅᑦᑕᕐᒪᑦ ᒪᒃᑯᒃᑑᖅᑎᒥᓂ. ᐋᑦᑕᐃᔭᖅᑐᕌᒻᒪᑕᔫᖅ ᐊᖅᓴᙳᐊᖅᑐᕌᒻᒪᑕ ᐃᓚᒌᓕᖅᑐᖅᓗᑎᒃ ᐊᑯᖅᓯᒋᐊᖅᑕᖅᓗᑎᒃ, ᑕᐃᒃᑯᐊ ᐊᑯᖅᓯᒐᕋᒃᑐᖅᑕᑦ ᓵᓚᒃᓴᖅᑕᖅᓗᑎᒃ ᐃᓚᒌᑦ. ᑕᐃᒪᔫᖅ ᑕᐃᒻᓇ ᓂᕈᐊᖅᓯᐊᖅ ᐱᙳᐊᓗᐊᖅᑐᖅᑕᐅᔭᒌᖕᒐᑦ ᐊᓐᓗᒌᖕᒋᔫᖅ ᐊᓚᒃᑐᒐᐅᑦᑕᖅᑲᑦᑖᒥᐊᕋᒻᒪᑕ ᓵᓚᒋᔭᐅᓗᐊᑦᑎᐊᒥᐊᖅᑕᖅᑲᑦᑖᖅᒪᑦ ᐹᔭᑦᓗᒃᑐᒐᐅᖅᑦᓗᓐᓈᒥᐊᖅᐸᒃᓗᓂ. ᐊᓈᓇᑦᓯᐊᖕᒐᔫᖅ ᓱᓇᐃᑦᑑᒐᒥ ᑐᐱᕐᒥᓂᑦ

There was an old woman who lived alone with her teenaged granddaughter. They were outcasts. The old woman was too old to move around, so she stayed mostly around her tent. Her granddaughter was young and she would play with the other young people. They used to make balls out of skin filled with sand to play a game called "aataijaq." They had two teams, and they threw the ball up in the air. The group that caught the ball the most won.

Every time they played, the girl's clothes would be torn and her

ᓅᑦᑐᐃᑦᑑᒐᒥ ᐊᓐᓄᕌᒃᑲᓂᒃ ᐱᑕᖅᑲᖕᒋᓐᓇᒥ ᐊᓐᓄᕌᖕᒋᒎᖅ ᒥᖅᑯᖅᐸᒃᓱᒋᑦ ᐊᓕᖕᓂᑯᐃ ᐱᑦᑕᖅᑲᑦᑖᕋᒥᐅᒃ. ᐊᓕᒃᑕᓕᓂᔾᔪᐊᕐᒥᒎᖅ ᒥᑭᓪᓕᖕᒪᑕ ᒥᖅᑯᖅᑕᖅᑲᑦᑳᓗᐊᓕᕐᒪᒋᑦ ᐊᑎᒐᐃᓯᑎᒥᐊᓕᕐᒪᑦ ᓂᖕᒐᐃᔫᒥᔪᖅ ᑎᐊᓐᓇ ᐱᓴᐅᒐᔪᓗᐊᓕᕐᒪᑦ.

ᑕᐃᒪᒎᖅ ᓇᑦᓯᐅᑉ ᓂᐊᕐᑯᐊᓂᒃ ᐊᒥᐊᓂᒃ ᓇᑲᓯᒪᔪᒥᒃ ᓱᓇᒋᖕᔪᒍᑭᐊᖅ ᐱᖅᑲᕐᓂᕋᒥ ᑭᓂᐅᖅᓯᖅᓱᒍᒎᖅ ᑭᓂᖕᒪᖕᒎᖅ ᐆᒃᑐᖅᑕᖅᓱᒍ ᐃᖖᒍᑕᕐᒥ ᓂᐊᕐᑯᐊᓄᑦ ᓇᓴᖅᓱᒍ ᐃᓰᑎᒍᑦ ᑕᐅᑐᓕᖅᓱᓂ ᐊᒻᒪ ᖃᓂᐊᒍᑦ

grandmother would sew them when she got home. The other players would bully her, and they tore her clothes often, but her grandmother had no new skins to use to repair them. So, she would simply sew the torn pieces together. The girl's clothes were ripped and mended so often that they became too small for her. This was greatly upsetting to her grandmother, as she did not have any skins to make her more clothes.

One day, the old woman found a seal's head and used it to make a mask that fit the girl very well.

ᐊᓂᖅᑳᓴᖅᑐᓕᖅᓱᓂ, ᕿᓯᒃ ᑕᐃᒪ ᓇᑦᓯᐅᑉ ᓂᐊᖁᐊ ᖃᓂᖅᑲᖅᓱᓂ ᐃᔨᖅᑲᖅᓂᖅᒪᑦ. ᑎᐊᓐᓇᒎᖅ ᐊᑎᔾᔪᒍ ᓇᑦᓯᐅᔮᓕᕈᑎᖅᑲᖅᓱᓂ ᓇᓴᖅᑕᖅᒪᒍ. ᓇᓴᖅᓯᓐᓇᖅᓱᒍᒎᖅ ᐹᒍᑕᓐᓈᖅᑲᕋᒥᒎᖅ ᐃᓄᐃᑦ ᐹᒍᑖᑦ ᐊᓪᓚᕋᖅ. ᕿᔫᓇᓪᓇᐊᕐᒥᔪᖅ ᕿᔪᖕᓂᒃ ᐹᒍᑕᖅᑲᔪᓚᐅᕐᒪᑕ.
ᑕᐃᑯᓐᖓᒎᖅ ᐃᒻᒥᖅᓱᒍ ᐊᑦᖃᐅᒪᑎᑦᑕᕐᒪᒍ ᐃᖦᔭᙳᓕᕌᖓᒥ ᒪᑭᓐᓂᓗᒃᑲᓗᐊᕌᖓᑦ ᒪᑭᑎᓐᓂᓗᖕᓇᓵᓂᓗᒃᑎᑦᑕᖅᓱᒍ. ᐊᔪᓕᓕᖅᑯᕌᖓᖕᒎᖅ ᐳᐃᑎᑦᑕᖅᓱᒍ ᐃᓛ ᓄᐃᑎᑦᑕᕐᒪᒍ ᐊᓂᖅᑳᓕᓵᖅᑕᕐᒪᑦ. ᑕᐃᒪ

It fit her so well that she was able to see out through the eye holes and breathe through the hole of the mouth. She looked very much like a seal.

The grandmother owned a small wooden storage box. She filled the box up with water. She then trained her granddaughter to hold her breath underwater. She would only allow her to come up for air when she was feeling light-headed.

Once she was able to hold her breath for a long period of time, the grandmother told her, "The next time the young people are playing, do not

ᓯᖅᑐᕐᓂᕋᐃᓱᕋᑉᑕ ᐊᓂᖅᑳᓇᓵᒍᔪᔾᔪᐊᕐᓂᒃ ᐊᓂᖅᑳᖅᑕᐃᓕᔾᔪᓂᒃ. ᐊᖅᑲᐅᒪᕐᑲᑦᑕᔪᓯᔪᔾᔫᒪᖕᒎᖅ ᑎᐊᓐᓇᐃᓕᐅᖅᑕᕐᑲᑦᑖᕐᒪᒍ ᐅᖅᑲᐅᑎᔮ. “ᑕᐃᒃᑯᐊ ᐱᙳᐊᑦᑐᐊᓕᕐᒥᒃᐸᑕ ᐱᙳᐊᓇᐊᖅᑐᖅᑲᑕᐅᖕᒋᓪᓗᑎᑦ ᑕᓴᒨᓇ ᓯᒡᔭᒧᑦ ᐃᒫᕐᓗᑎᑦ ᐸᐃᖕᔭᕐᓗᑎᑦ ᓵᖕᒐᓄᓕᐊᕐᓗᑎᑦ ᑕᑯᑎᓐᓂᓗᒍᒫᖅᐸᑎᑦ ᓇᑦᓯᐅᓯᖅᑐᕐᓗᑎᑦ. ᖃᐅᔨᑎᓐᓂᓗᓕᕈᖕᓂ ᓯᕐᑭᖅᐸᓚᒃᔪᐊᓇᐊᖅᑕᕐᓗᑎᑦ ᐊᖅᑲᖅᐸᓪᓚᓗᒥᐊᑦᑐᐊᕐᓗᑎᑦ ᖃᐅᔨᑉᐸᑕ ᓇᑦᓯᓕᓇᒥᐊᕈᒫᕐᓇᓇᐊᕐᒪᑕ ᑕᒻᒫᔭᕐᓗᑎᒃ ᓇᑦᓯᐅᓱᒋᓗᑎᑦ.”

to join them. Instead, go out into the water, but be sure that they can spot you. Make noises and they will come out to try to catch you, as they will think that you are a seal.”

The girl did as she was told.

As soon as she began swimming, someone did spot her and yelled, “A seal!” So, they all ran to their qajaqs and went out to sea, thinking that she was a real seal.

Whenever they approached her, she would dive under and encourage

ᑕᑯᕋᖅᑲᓐᓕᐊᕐᒪᖕᒍᖅ ᓇᓕᕆᕐᕋᐊᓂᐊᑐᖅᑲᕐᕋᐊᓕ
ᐊᖅᐸᓪᒐᓇᐊᕐᐊᒐᑐᐊᖅᑐᓐᑭ ᖃᕐᕀᒥᐊᓄᒃ. ᖃᕐᕀᓗᖅᐸᒃᖃᖕᒍᖅ ᒪᓐᑲᖅᓗᑕ
ᑕᐊᑦᕀᒥᖕᒐ ᐃᓅᐊᓂᕐᒥ ᓇᕐᕀᕀᒥᕀᕐᕙᒍ. ᖃᕐᕀᑕᓯᖕᕀᑯᒐᖅ ᐊᖅᒃᖅᐸᑦᑐᓂ
ᕀᐃᐊᓇᖅᕀᕐᐊᒍᖕᒍᖅ ᐳᐃᑦᑕᐅᕀᕐᓄᓂ ᑕᓲᕀᒐ ᕀᕐᕈᓚᐃᑎᑦᒐᖕᒍᖅ.
ᐊᓇᑦᕀᐊᕐᒐ ᐅᖅᑲᐅᑕᑕᐅᕐᒐᒐ ᕀᕐᕈᐅᑕᕐᕐᒐᖕᒍᖅ ᓄᖃ ᐅᕐᒧᕀᕀᕀᕐᑕ
ᐱᓇᐊᑐᒧᒐᖅᖚᖅ ᑎᐊᓂ ᐅᖅᑲᕐᓄᓂ, "ᐅᕀ.....ᕀᑐᒍ ᓇᐅᕐ," ᑎᐊᓇᒍᖅ
ᐱᕀᐃᑐᐊᖅᐸᔾᕐ ᐊᓄᓇ ᑎᕐᕐᓂᐊᕐᕋᕐ. ᑕᐱᒪᒍᖅ ᓄᖃ ᐅᕐᒧᕀᕀᕀᒪᕐ

the hunters to follow her farther out to sea.

Her grandmother had instructed her to take them out to the open sea. She was then to instruct the wind to stir and strengthen by shouting, "Uugaa . . . where is my wind?"

So, when she had lured the people far enough away from shore, she shouted as her grandmother had instructed her. As soon as she did, a strong north wind picked up, savagely blowing the men out to sea.

The men in the qajaqs struggled with the winds. They tried to keep

ᐅᒡᒍᔾᔭᐊᕋᓗᐊᖅᖢᒍᒎᖅ ᑕᒪᔾᔭᐊᕐᒥᒎᖅ ᐳᓯᓯᓐᓇᕈᒫᓕᖅᑰᒪᓂᒃ ᓴᑉᑯᒥᐊᕐᒪᒍ ᐊᒡᒍᒧᑦ ᐊᔭᓕᕋᒥᒃ ᐊᑉᕐᑯᓇᖅᑭᐅᑎᐊᒥᐊᓕᕋᒥᒃ ᐳᓯᑦᑕᓗᕐᑭᑦᖢᑎᒎᖅ ᖃᔭᐃᑦ ᐊᖑᑎᔾᔭᐃᑦ ᐃᐱᐅᕋᓚᐅᕐᒪᑕ. ᑕᐃᒃᑯᐊᒎᖅ ᒪᑦᕈᑐᐊᓐᓈᒃ ᑭᕕᐅᕐᓗ ᓄᑲᓖᖑᓚᐅᓂᕐᒪᓂᒃ ᐳᓯᓐᓇᓵᖅᑐᑕᐅᓚᐅᕐᒪᓂᒃ. ᓇᓕᐊᑭᐊᖅ ᓄᑲᖅᓱᕐᓘᕝᕙ ᐳᓯᑉᐹᒃᑕᓕᕐᒥᒪᖖᒎᖅ ᑭᕕᐅᒻᖑᖅ ᑎᒍᒻᒥᓂᓗᒃᑕᓚᐅᕋᓗᐊᕐᒪᒍ ᐳᓯᖃᑕᐅᑉᐹᒃᑕᓕᕐᒪᑦ ᑕᐃᑉᓱᒪᒎᖅ ᓄᑲᓕᓇᓪᓕᐊᒑᓘᕝᕙ ᐊᖓᔭᐊᓘᕝᕙ ᐅᖃᐅᑎᕚ, “ᐳᓯᖃᑕᐅᓯᓐᓇᑦᑐᐊᓕᕐᕋᕗᑎᑦ ᐃᓱᒪᒋᖖᒋᒥᐊᓕᖖᒐ,”

their qajaqs upright, but many of them capsized and eventually drowned.

Finally, there were two men left who had not capsized. They were Kiviuq and his younger brother.

Kiviuq took his brother’s qajaq and desperately tried to keep it from sinking, but his brother told him to let go, otherwise they both may not survive.

Although he did not want his brother to die, Kiviuq had no choice

ᐅᒡᒍᓇᕙᐊᖁᓗᐊᖅᓗᒍᒍᒎᖅ ᑕᒪᔾᔪᐊᕐᒥᒎᖅ ᐸᓯᓯᓐᓇᕈᓖᓕᖅᑰᒪᓂᒃ ᓴᑉᑯᒥᐊᕐᒪᒍ ᓴᑉᑯᓈᑐᐊᕐᒪᒍᒎᖅ ᐸᓯᓐᓇᒥ ᑐᕐᑯᖅᑕᐅᓕᖅᓗᓂ.

ᑕᐃᒪᓇᒎᖅ ᑭᕕᐅᖅ ᐊᑕᐅᓯᑦᑎᐊᒥᐊᖑᓕᕐᒥ ᐸᓯᑦᑕᐃᓕᐅᔭᓐᓈᖅᓗᓂ ᑎᖅᑲᐅᔭᒥᐊᓕᕐᒪᑦ ᐊᑉᕐᑯᓇᑦᑎᐊᒥᐊᕐᒪᑦ.

but to let go. As soon as he did, his brother's qajaq sank below the waves and disappeared.

Kiviuq was the only one who survived.

ᑐᑉᑕᐊ • Part Two

ᑕᒪᖅᑐᑦ ᑕᓄᐅᒥ • Lost at Sea

ᐃᑲᔮᖅᑎᖃᔭᑕᐅᒪᖕᒐᑐᔪᖅ ᓯᓇᒥᐊᓂᖕ, ᑭᕕᐅᖅ ᓴᖕᕿᒐᖕ
ᐃᑲᔮᖅᑎᖃᔭᖕᓂᖕᒐᖕ ᑕᐃᒪᓇᒃᔪᖕ ᓴᖕᕿᖄᖕ ᖃᕿᑕ ᓯᑍᖕᖕᐊᓂ ᓄᐸᐊᓂ
ᒥᖕᒃᐃᖕᐃᖕᓇᖕᓂᖕᒐᖕ ᐳᕿᖕᑎᖄᐃᖕᓂᖅᑐᖅ. ᑕᑦᖁᓂᔪᖅ ᐃᑭᐅᖄᐅᕆᐊᖅᑐ ᓂ
ᑕᖕᓚᓂᔪᖅ ᓄᓇᑕᐊᑐᕿᕿᒐᖃ ᐊᖕᖅᑭᕿᒥᕿᐊᓂᖕᓚ ᓄᓇ ᑕᑐᑐᔪᖁᓇᐃᕿᐳᖕ
ᑕᒪᖁᓚᖕᔪᖅ ᓄᓇᖕ ᓇᕿᓂᖕ ᖃᑭᖅᔭᖕᓇᖃᐃᕿᓚ. ᐃᕿᑲᕿᖕᑎᐊᕿᐊᕿᕿᒐ ᔪᖅ
ᐅᖅᕿᐊᖕᑎᐊᕿᐊᕿᓚ ᐊᓄᖄᖕᒪᓂᐅᕿᓚ ᓯᓂᑕᐳᖄᕿᓚᖁᔪᖕ
ᑕᐃᒪᓇᔪᖅ ᐃᑲᔮᖅᑎᓇᖕᒃ ᓴᖕᕿᖄᖅ ᖃᖄᐅᑉ ᓯᑍᖕᐊᓂᖕᑐᖅ

Kiviuq drifted away, but tried to keep the qajaq stable at the same time.

He had a spirit helper, a sandpiper with a red line around its neck. The bird sat at the front of the qajaq, preventing it from capsizing. Kiviuq was all alone, drifting out to sea all by himself. There was no land to be seen.

Eventually, he became very tired. The waters had become calm, so he told his spirit helper, "I'm going to take a nap, so I need you to be on the lookout for me."

ᐅᖅᑯᐱᑎᒐᖅᑐᓂᐅᑉ ᓯᓇᐊᑦᓕᕆᐊᓯᒐᕐᒪ ᒥᐊᓂᑕᐅᖢᐸᕐᖓᖅᑐᒍ.
ᓯᓇᖅᑦᑦᐊᖏᓗᐊᓯᖔᔪᖅ ᐳᓴᕐᑑᓄᓂᖃᖅ ᑐᐸᖕᒥᐊᖅ.
    ᑐᐸᖅᒪᑦᕋᒥᔪᖅ ᐃᖅᐊᕐᔪᖕᖑᐃᕐᒥ ᓄᓇᕐᐅᖅᑐᓂ
ᐊᐸᓯᖅᑕᕐᐊᓕᖏᓕᑦ ᒎᖕᒥᕐᐊᖅ ᓯᖅᓂᖅ ᓇᓄᓇᐃᖃᑕᖅᕐᔪᒍ
ᑐᓄᐊᓂᖅᒪᑦᕋᕐᔪᖢᑦ ᓯᖅᓂᖅ ᐅᐃᒪᕐᖔᖑᐃᕐᒥᔪᖅ ᓯᖅᓂᔪᖅᕐᖅ
ᖁᑦᑎᖅᕐᖅᖓᕐᒪᑦ ᑐᓂᕐᒍ ᐊᐅᖅᕐᒪᑦᕋᓯᕐᒥ ᓯᓇᐅᕐᔪᖅ
ᓄᓇᐃᓯᐊᕐᓯᖏᒪᑦ, ᐊᓄᕋᐃᓕᒪᔪᖅ ᐅᖅᑯᐊᕐᑎᐊᕐᐊᖅᑕᖅᕐᑐᔪᖅ.

Although he had taken a very long, deep sleep, when Kiviuq awoke the qajaq had not capsized. He was amazed by this.

He began his journey to look for land using the sun as a guide.

Whenever the sun was high, he would turn his back to it and begin paddling.

At last he thought he saw land, only to find out that it was a mirage. This happened a number of times. In his desperation to reach land, he started hallucinating. Kiviuq wanted to reach land so badly that he began imagining it.

ᓄᓇᐅᔭᖅᑐᒥᒃ ᑕᑯᖡᒍᐊᡕᐦᒥᒌ ᑕᖠᖅᑕᑕᐅᒐᒪᑕ ᖅᐸᐱᖅ ᓘᑎᑭᐊᖅ
ᑕᐅᑐᖅᑯᖅᒥᑕᐦᖅᑐᡖᓂᖅᑦᒐᦲᒻᔫᖅ ᓄᓇᒧᐊᑉᐊᑐᐊᒍᖅ. ᑕᐱᒻᒍᖅ
ᑭᖡᒐᑦᑕᖅᐸᖡᒐᑦᖅᑐᒥᒃ ᓄᓇᔫᖅᑐᒥᒃ ᑕᑯᒻᒪᒃ ᐅᖅᖃᖡ ᓄᓂᒌᖅ; "ᑕᖃᐸᒪ
ᓄᓇᐅᕆᓴᒍᐊᑎᐳᖅ ᓄᖅᒣᓈᓂᐊᒐᐦᑎᐊᑎᐳᖅᖅ," ᓄᓇᔫᓂᖅᒪᒫᔫᖅ
ᖅᑭᒨᒣᑕᖅᒍᓂ.

ᓄᓇᒧᑕᐊᒐᒣᔫᖅ ᖅᑿᓂ ᖅᑐᐃᑦᑕᓂᕐᔭᐊᒐᖅᑭ ᐃᒻᒪᖡᓂᖅᓄᒫᐦᒑᕱ
ᖅᑐᐃᑦᑕᒪᕱᒫᒐᕱ ᐃᑐᐊᓄᕱ, ᐳᕆᕿᐊᖡᒇᕱᐊᑕᖡᓈᒐᕝ. ᐃᒪᓂᐴᑎᖡᓂᖅᒪᒫᔫᖅ

He continued on and on and eventually did come across land. At first
he did not believe it was real and said, "It looks like land, but it will probably
fade again."

When he realized it was solid land, he became happy and relaxed.

The first thing that he had to do was drain the urine from the qajaq.

He drained the urine through the back. Qajaqs had holes in the back
that were used to drain water. These could be plugged when the qajaq was in
use.

ᖁᐃᑕᕐᓂᑯᐊᓂᒃ ᐃᑭᐅᑐᐃᓇᒥᐊᖅᑐᓂ ᑎᐊ'ᓇᒥᐊᖅ ᖁᐃᑕᒥᐊᕐᓂᕐᒪᑦ. ᑯᕕᑎᖅᑳᖅᑐᒍᒎᖅ ᑯᕕᕝᕕᖅᑲᐅᔭᔪᓚᐅᕐᒪᑕ ᑭᖑᓂᐊᒍᑦ ᓯᒥᒃᑕᖅᑐᒍ. ᑯᕕᑎᖅᑳᖅᑐᒍᒎᖅ ᐃᒪᐃᕈᑎᒻᒪᑦ ᑎᒡᕗᓇᐊᓈᖅᑐᒍ ᑭᖖᒐᓐᓈᓗᖖᒎᖅ ᒪᔪᖅᑐᓂ ᓇᓯᑦᑕᖅᑐᒥᐊᖅᑐᓂᐅᒐᓗᐊᖅ ᑳᒻᒫᖅᑐᓂ ᐃᒥᕈᒃᑐᔾᔫᒐᒥᒎᖅ ᐃᒪᖅᓯᐅᓗᒃᑑᒐᓗᐊᖅ, ᐃᒥᕈᑦᑎᐊᒥᐊᓕᕐᒪᖕᒎᖅ ᑕᒻᒪᐅᒪᓕᓂᖕᒥᒃ. ᖃᔭᓂ ᐃᑦᑐᐊᖅᑭᓯᓐᓇᖅᑐᒍ ᐃᒥᖅᓯᐅᓗᕆᐊᕐᒪᑦ. ᖄᖕᒐᓗᐊᕆᒥᒎᖅ ᖃᓂᑉᐹᑐᐃᓐᓇᖕᒥᒃ ᑐᐱᖕᒥᒃ ᑕᓯᕋᓐᓈᒻᒎᖅ ᑕᓯᖅᔪᐊᓈᑉ ᓯᓈᓂ

He docked his qajaq and began walking over a small hill. He went looking for animals and some fresh water, as he was very thirsty.

The first thing he did was look for water, as he had been lost for a long time. There, next to a lake, he saw a lone tent.

He wondered why there was only one tent. He began walking toward it.

He got to the doorway of the tent and made a small opening and took a peek inside.

There, on the bed, he saw two women. They looked frightened; they

ᑐᕕᖕᒥᕐ ᑕᑯᔪᕐᔪᐃᓪᓕᑦ, ᖅᑭᖅᑕᑕᒪᓗᑎᐊᒡᒪᔾᔾᖅ ᠂ᑉᕝ ᑐᕕᖅᑕᒃᑲᒻᓚ᠂ᒡᑦ
ᐃᓯᒻᒥᖕᕓᔾᔪᐊᕐᒡᑎᐅᒡ. ᑕᐊᑯᖕᒪᔾᖅ ᐅᕐᓂᒻᐊᒡᒍ ᐃᓄᖅᖏᑦᕐᑘᕓᐊᕐᒡᑦ
ᓂᐸᐃᖃᐅᕝᕓᐊᖅᓂᖅᒪᓄᖕ ᒪᒡᖝᖁᓈ᠂ᓐ ᐊᖃᐃᓄᕝᕋᐊᖅ ᐸᓂᒥᔪᖠᓇᕑᖅᑐᑎᒻᔾᖅ.
ᐃᓚᓇᒥᔾᖅ ᕓᖕᒪ ᐸᑭᖕᓂᐊᖅᑑᒡ ᐃᑕᑐᐊᑎᐊᒡᒪᑦ ᐃᕝᑯᐊᒡᒥᔾᖅ ᐃᖕᑕᕐᒥ
ᑐᖕᖃᓂᕐᒥ᠂ᔾᖁᕐᕓᖅ ᐱᔾᖅᕝ᠂ᖕᑎᒻᕐ ᕓᒧᖕᒋᖅ ᑕᐅᑐᐣᖃᖅᑐᔾᕝᕓᐊ
ᕓᓄᕝᒔᐊᓄᕐ. ᑕᐃᒪᒍᔾᖅ ᑕᕝᕋᖅ ᐃᓯᒻᒥᖕᑎᔾᒍ ᐃᒻᖃᐢᒪᓂᔾᖅ
ᐃᒻᐅᕐᐃᖅᖅᓂᖅᒪᓄᖕ, ᑭᐊᐅᖅ ᐊᖃᖅᑐᐊᖁᑦᑉ ᐅᖃᖅᑐᖅ. "ᖅ᠂᠂᠂ᑉᑕᐊᒻᐊᖅ

had heard him coming. They were mother and daughter.

He forgot about the water in the lake, because the women had some water already. Kiviuq said to the mother, "I have not been on land for a long time and I'm very thirsty. Would you allow me to drink some of your water?"

The woman replied, "Only if you agree to become my son-in-law will you have a drink." He did not want to marry the daughter.

Kiviuq repeated his request. The older woman replied again, "Only if

ᓄᓇᒧᐊᔭᐃᖁᒪ ᐸᓐᓇᐃᓕᖁᒪ ᐅᕙᖓᑦ ᐃᒥᓈᕐᓚᖓ." ᑕᓯᖁᑮᖅ ᐃᓱᒪᕆᖕᕆᓗᒍ ᑕᐃᑉᓱᒥᖓ ᐃᒥᐅᑖᓂᒃ ᐃᒥᕈᐊᖅᑕᒪᑦ. ᑕᐃᒻᓇᒎᖅ ᐊᕐᓇᕐᑯᐊᒃᓵᓈᖅ ᐅᖅᑲᖅᓯᓐᓇᓱᖕᒐᔭᖕᒪᑦ. "ᓂᖓᐅᑖᕆᓂᐊᓂᕈᑉᐱᑦ ᑭᓯᐊᓂ ᐃᒥᕐᓂᐊᖅᑐᑎᑦ." ᓇᑦᓚᑳᖅᑭᔭᐊᓕᖁᓗᐊᖅᑯᓂᒎᖅ ᓂᖓᐅᑖᕆᔭᐅᓱᐊᖕᕆᑲᓗᐊᒻᒦᖅᑯᓂ. "ᐃᓛ ᐸᓐᓇᐃᓕᓗᐊᕚᒃᑲᒪᐃᓛ ᖃᖓᔾᔭᐊᖅ ᓄᓇᒧᐊᔭᐃᖁᒪ ᐃᒥᓈᕐᓚᖓ." "ᐊᓱᒎᖅ ᓂᖓᐅᑖᕆᓂᐊᕐᓂᕈᑉᐱᑦ ᑭᓯᐊᓂ ᐃᒥᕐᓂᐊᖅᑐᑎᑦ." ᐊᖕᕆᒥᐊᑦᑐᐊᖅᑯᓂᒎᖅ ᐃᒥᕈᑦᑎᐊᓪᓗᐊᕚᒥᐊᖁᒥ ᐃᒥᒥᐊᕐᒪᑦ ᓂᖓᐅᑖᕆᔫᒎᖅ.

you agree to become my son-in-law."

Again he pleaded, "Please allow me to have a drink. I have not had a drink for a very long time."

Finally, Kiviuq agreed to become the old woman's son-in-law because he was so thirsty. So he drank, and became her son-in-law.

Kiviuq was the only man at the camp, and so he became the hunter.

The island they camped on was very close to the mainland, so he was able to hunt caribou.

ᓴᐱᕐᑖᓯᓂᐅᒍᖅ ᐊᖁᕐᖁᐊᖃᖃᖅ ᐊᖢᑕᐱᑦᒪᓂᖅ
ᒪᖁᐱᖢᑏᖁᓂᖁᒪᓂᖅ ᖁᑭᖅᑕᒌᑐᒥᐊᓗᓂᖅᑐᖏᑦ. ᑖᖁᓂᒍᖅ ᓄᓇ
ᖃᓂᑐᖀᓪᒪᒪᓪᓕᖅ ᓄᓇᖢᑐᐊᐱᖅ. ᖁᑭᖅᑕᒥ ᑐᐱᖅᒪᒪᓂᖅ ᓄᓇᒻᑕᐊᖅᑐᓂᒍᖅ
ᒪᖁᐱᑕᑦᓕᖢᒡᓕᖅ ᑐᖅᑐᐸᖅᑐᓂᓗ ᓯᐊᒥᐊᓂᖅ ᓂᖁᖃᖁᖅ ᑕᓂᐱᑐ
ᐳᐃᖀᓂᖅ ᐅᖢᖅᓇᖣᖒᓂᖅ ᓇᖁᖅᖣᖣᖒᓂᖅ ᐱᑕᖅᑕᖅᑐᓂ ᑕᐃᖁᒪᓂ
ᐊᑕᑦᖅᑯᑕᐸᑐᖁᐊᖁᒪᖁ ᐊᐱᖁᐊᖁᖁᖁᐊᑕᖁᕐᒎᖅ ᐱᒪᒪᖁᖔᐳᑕᖅᐳᖅ.
ᑲᒥᑲᒍ ᐃᖢᐃᒥᓂᖅ ᑕᒪᒪᐱᖁᖅᑖᖅᐸᒪᓂ ᐊᒪᓪ ᐳᐊᒍᐃᑕ ᐃᖢᐃᒥᓂᖅ

He would also hunt sea mammals. But he was becoming homesick.
He came up with a plan that he would one day leave his new family
and go home. So, when he went hunting, he pretended to lose a mitt and
a kamik (one skin boot), hiding these items under rocks on the mainland.
This continued for some time. Every time he would return home, his wife
would have to make him a new mitt and a new kamik. Kiviuq was hiding all
of his extra mitts and kamiks (so that he would have enough equipment for
the long journey when he eventually left).

ᑕᒻᒪᐠᓯᖅᑐᖅᐸᑯᓄ ᑎᑭᑦᑎᖅᑲᑦᑕᓐᖑᓪᓪᑦ. ᑕᐊᓇᒍᖕ ᓄᑕᐊᖕ
ᓂᕕᐊᖅᑭᐊᔨᓪᑦ ᓘᑯᒃᑐᓕᒧᒐᒥᓪᑦ ᑎᑭᓴᖅᑐᑦᓐᖑᓐᖑᖕᔅ ᓯᖕᔪᒋᐊᖅᑲᑦᑕᔨᓪᑦ
ᓂᐅᕐᐊᕿᖅᑐᖅᑐᓄ ᐱᑕᐃᓂᖅ, ᖃᔨᑕ ᖃᒥᐊᖕᓄ ᐱᖂᑕᐃᒧ ᐱᑕᐃᒧ
ᐅᕐᓕᒡᒫᑦ ᑎᐊᖅᖃ ᖃᔨᐊᑦ ᐅᕐᕐᒧᐳᖕᒪᑦ.

ᑕᒪᒍᖕ ᖃᓇ ᐊᕐᖃᒡᐊᑉᑲᖃᖕ ᓯᖕᔪᑯᐊᕐᐊᑦᑐᒧᐅᖅᑉᖃᖕᓄ
ᑭᖕᒧᑦᓐᖅᐻᔪᑦᓐᖓ ᓘᖅᑲᐃᑦᖕᑎᕐᔾᑯ ᐳᐊᓄᐃᖅᑲᖅᑭᖅᑐᑉᖃᖕᓄᓄ
ᑲᖕᖅᑲᖅᑲᖅᑐᑉᖃᖕᓄ ᑲᑎᖅᑯᑦᐃᐊᕐᒥᐅᖕᒧᒥᖕᒧᐊᓐᖃᓐᒥ

When hunting by qajaq, the hunter places the catch on top of the qajaq. The young wife would always meet Kiviuq at the beach to help with his catch.

The mother would never normally go to the beach to meet Kiviuq. But, on his last hunting trip, the mother met him at the beach.

While Kiviuq was out hunting, she had killed her daughter by piecing her ear with a sharp object when she was pretending to pick lice from her hair. That killed her instantly, and she had done this so that she could

ᓴᐅᑦᑕᖅᔪᒋᑦ ᐱᕿᓱᑦᑕᓗᒋᓪᓘᕙ. ᑭᖑᓕᖅᐹᒥᒎᖅ ᒪᖅᑲᐃᓕᖅᒥᒐᒥ ᐊᐃᓕᖅᒪᖒᖅ ᑕᐃᒻᓇᒎᖅ ᐊᕐᓇᕐᑯᐊᒃᑳᔾᓴᐊᖅ ᐸᓂᖕᒥᓂᒃ ᐊᖅᓵᖅᓯᓂᓗᒃᑐᑯᓂᔾᓵᓕᕐᓂᕐᒥ ᑐᕐᑯᓐᓂᖅᔪᓂᐅᒎᖅ ᐸᓂᓂ. ᑯᒪᐃᖅᓯᖅᑐᖅᔪᒍᒎᖅ ᒪᓂᒻᒥᑕᕐᒪᑦ ᓯᐅᑖᒍᖖᒎᖅ ᓱᓇᒧᒃᑭᐊᖅ ᑲᐱᒻᒪᒍ ᑐᕐᑯᓴᔾᓵᒻᒪᑦ, ᓯᐅᑖᑕ ᐃᓗᐊᒍᑦ ᑲᐱᔭᒥᐊᔾᓴᐊᖓ. ᑐᕐᑯᒻᒪᖖᒎᖅ ᑮᓈᒎᖅ ᐋᒃᑐᖅᔪᓂᐅᒃ ᑕᐃᒻᓇᐅᓯᖅᑐᖅᑐᓵᓕᕐᓂᕐᒪᑦ. ᓯᒡᔭᒧᓕᐊᖅᑐᖀᖅ ᑭᕕᐅᑉ ᑕᑯᒐᒥᐅᒃ ᓄᓕᐊᕆᖏᒻᒪᒍᒎᖅ ᓇᓗᓇᖏᑐᔾᔪᓵᒐᓗᐊᕐᒪᑦ ᓯᖏᓯᖅᑐᖅᔪᓂ.

become Kiviuq's wife. She took the skin of her daughter's face and made a mask. Pretending to be her daughter, the old woman went down to meet Kiviuq as he approached the shore.

Kiviuq saw her walking to the beach. He knew that she was not his wife, but he did not make this known to her.

She got to the beach and yelled to Kiviuq, giving him directions so that he could set his qajaq safely.

Kiviuq knew that she was not his wife. He yelled to her, "Take off

ᓯᒡᔭᒦᓗᓂᒎᖅ ᑐᖅᓗᓛᓱᖕᒐᔭᓚᖅᒪᑦ ᑎᑭᓴᖅᑐᓚᖅᒪᑦ. "ᐅᕝᕙ ᐅᕝᕙ ᓯᒡᔭᓇᖕᓂᖅᑳᑎᐊᖅ," ᑎᐊᓐᓇᒎᖅ ᐅᖅᑲᖅᑕᓚᖅᒪᑦ ᓇᓗᕆᖕᕆᓇᒥᐅᒎᖅ ᑕᐃᒻᓇᐅᖕᕆᒪᑦ ᑐᖅᓗᓚᔮᒎᖅ, "ᑲᒥᓪᓚᓗᑎᑦ." ᑲᒥᓪᓚᐸᑦᓲᒪᖖᒎᖅ ᑲᓈᓐᓈᕆᖖᒎᖅ ᑐᐊᑦᑐᒐᔮᒃ. ᐊᖅᓇᖅᑯᐊᒃᑲᓗᔾᔫᒐᒥᒎᖅ ᑲᓈᖅᓗᒃᑐᒐᔮᒃ, ᑲᒪᓱᐸᑦᓲᒪᖖᒎᖅ ᐊᓱᒎᕉᓂᓛ ᓄᓕᐊᓂᖕᕆᑖ ᑲᓈᖅᓗᒃᑐᒐᔫᒃ ᑕᑯᒻᒪᒍ.

ᓯᒡᔭᒧᖖᒎᖅ ᑐᓚᒫᖕᒐᒥ ᖃᔮᒎᖅ ᓴᓐᓂᖅᓗᒍ ᐱᑦᑕᕈᒻᒪᑦ ᓯᒡᔭᓇᖕᓂᓈᒧᑦ. ᓂᐅᓯᕆᐊᖅᑯᓚᖅᒪᒍᒎᖅ ᑕᐃᒻᓇᒎᖅ ᓄᓕᐊᖕᒐ ᑐᒃᑐᐃᑦ

your kamiks."

His suspicion was correct. She indeed was not his wife. Her old legs proved that.

When Kiviuq returned from hunting trips, he would paddle in and pull his qajaq in sideways.

Kiviuq's wife would have no problem in lifting and tossing his catch, so he asked the old lady to do the same.

ᐅᒃᐸᑏᓂᒃ ᐅᕘᓇ ᖁᖅᑐᕌᑕ ᓴᐅᓂᐊᒍᑦ ᑎᒍᐊᓪᓚᒥᐊᖅᕈᒋᑦ ᐃᒋᑦᑎᓱᕐᒪᑦ ᓄᓇᒧᑦ. ᑎᐊᓐᓇᒎᖅ ᖃᑭᑦᑎᒋᐊᖁᒻᒪᒍ ᓴᐱᓪᔩᑕᖅᑐᔾᔮᒻᒪᖖᒎᖅ ᖃᖕᒐᑦᑕᐃᓱᐃᑦᑐᖅ. ᖃᐅᔨᒪᖕᒋᓯᖅᑐᖅᕈᓂᐅᒎᖅ ᓄᓕᐊᕆᓯᖅᑐᕈᒻᒫᒐᔾᔭᐊᖅᕆᓕᒑ ᓇᓪᓕᒋᒥᐊᖅᕈᒍ. ᑕᐃᑯᖕᒐᒎᖅ ᐊᐃᒻᒪᓂᒃ ᑐᐱᕐᒧᐊᕐᒪᓂᒃ ᐊᐱᕆᔾᔭᕐᒪᒍᒎᖅ, “ᓇᐅᓪᓕ ᓄᓕᐊᕋ?” ᒪᓐᓂᑭᐅᓂᕋᖅᕈᓂᐅᒎᖅ ᓱᓇᐅᕙᒎᖅ ᐃᓗᕕᖅᑭᒪᓕᖅᑲᒻᒥᖕᒋᑦᑑᓐᓂᖅ. ᕿᓂᕐᓂᐊᓂᕋᖅᑭᑐᖅᕈᒍᒎᖅ ᑕᒫᓂ ᑐᐱᐅᑉ ᓴᓂᐊᓂ ᐱᓱᓘᔭᓕᕐᒪᑦ.

She was unable to lift the meat. This also confirmed that she was not his wife. Out of pity, he did not make this known to her.

When they got to the tent, Kiviuq asked the old woman where his wife was.

She answered that she was out egg picking. But really she had buried her already.

Kiviuq went out to take a walk and noticed his wife's grave, but he did

ᐃᓗᕕᖅᑭᓱᓚᐅᕐᒪᑕ ᐱᕉᒥᐊᖅᑐᕆᑦ, ᑕᐃᑲᐅᓐᓂᕐᑰᕐᒪᖕᒎᖅ ᑕᑯᓗᐊᖅᑐᓂᐅᒃ ᓱᖕᕆᓯᖅᑐᑦᑎᐊᒥᐊᖅᑐᓂ, ᐊᕐᓇᕐᑯᐊᒃᑳᓈᕉᖅ ᓴᑭᓂ ᓄᓚᐊᓇᐅᔭᓚᐅᒑ. ᐃᓱᒪᖅᓱᑦᑎᐊᓪᓚᓚᐅᖅᑳᖅᑐᒍᒎᖅ ᓱᓕᒎᖅ ᑲᒦᖅᓯᖅᑕᖅᑐᓂᓗ ᐳᐊᓗᐃᖅᓯᖅᑕᕐᒪᑦ. ᑕᐃᒻᓇᒎᖅ ᖃᐅᔨᕙᓪᓕᐊᔪᔾᔫᓕᖅᑯᕋᒥ ᑲᒦᖅᓯᖅᑐᓂᓘᕙ ᐳᐊᓗᐃᖅᓯᖅᑐᓂᓘᕙ ᑎᑭᒻᒥᖕᒪᑦ, ᐅᖅᑲᑉᐱᓘᔭᓐᓈᓱᖕᒐᔭᓕᕐᒪᑦ. “ᕿᒪᒍᒪᕙᓕᕋᖕᒪᖅᑳ ᑲᒦᕿᕿᖅᑐᖅᑎᓪᓗ ᐳᐊᓗᐃᕿᕿᖅᑐᑕᓪᓚᓕᖅᐱᑦ?” “ᕿᒪᓛᖕᒋᑭᑉᑭᑦ ᐱᓐᓇᕆᓚᕋᑉᑭᑦ,” ᓇᒡᓕᒋᓯᖅᑐᑦᓯᐊᒥᐊᖅᑐᒍᒎᖅ

not say anything. So they lived as husband and wife, although she was his mother-in-law.

One day, the old woman asked him if he was planning to leave her, because he would constantly return with a mitt or kamik missing, forcing her to constantly sew more.

He answered, “I will never leave you, I love you too much.”

ᑭᐅᑦᑕᐅᔭᒑ. "ᕿᒪᒍᒪᕙᓕᖕᓂᕈᖕᒪ ᓯᕗᖖᒋᑦ ᐃᓗᕿᐊᒃᑕᖃᖅᐳᖅ". "ᐊᓯᔫᖅ ᕿᒪᓚᖏᑭᑉᑭᑦ ᐱᓐᓇᓂᓴᖁᑉᑭᑦ."

ᑕᐃᒪᒎᖅ ᕿᒪᓪᓗᐊᕕᒋᐊᓕᕐᒥᐅᒎᖅ ᐊᐅᓪᓚᓗᐊᕕᔾᔪᐊᓕᕐᒪᑦ, ᑲᑉᐱᐊᒋᓕᓗᕿᔾᔪᒍ ᖃᓄᑭᐊᖅ ᐃᓱᒫᓗᓕᕐᒥ ᐊᐃᒋᐊᒥᐊᔾᔪᐊᓕᕐᒪᑦ.

She replied, "If you plan to leave me, you will be cursed, and face many challenges."

ᐱᖕᒪᖁᐊ • PART THREE

ᐊᖅᓯᑐᓂᖕᒪ • THE TRIALS

◁ᐅᑦᑕᖃᑎᖃᖅᑎᕐᲇᒍᔫᖅ ᓯᒻᕈᖅᑐ ᑎᑭᖅᑲᖅᑎᕐᲇᖰ
ᐊᖅᲇᐅᒍᔫᖅ ᐅᖃᑉᑎᕐᲇᕐᐊᕐᐋᕐᓂᖅ ᒪᓂᒃᕚᕐᒍᒐᕐᐋᕐᐋᕐᓂᖅ
ᐊᐳᖅᑭᒪᒃ ᐅᐃᕿᓇᐊᕐᲇᐊᕐᲇᖰᒍᔫᖅ ᕐᑐᓂᐊᓂ ᐃᓂᒪᒌᕐᲇᒡ
ᓄᑦᐊᕐᒌᐊᑯᲇᖅᖃᖅ ᲇᑎᔫᖅ ᕐᑕᐊᑎᖰᲇᓂᖅ ᐊᐅᑦᑕᖃᑐᖅ. ᑕᒪᒍᔫᖅ
ᐃᑲᓗᓂᕐᲇᑦ ᑐᑦᲇᒡᑦ ᐅᖅᑯᕐᲇᐊᕐᐃᕐᖅ ᑎᖅᑎᑦᒍᒐᕐᕐᲇᐊᕐᖅ ᐊᓂᕐᲇᖰᑐᒥᕚᕐᖅ.
ᐅᐃᕿᓇᐊᕐᲇᐊᕐᲇᖰᒍᔫᖅ ᑎᐊᖰᲇ ᕐᑐᓂᐊᐅᖰᖰᒪᒐᕐᐊᕐᖅᲇᖅᲇᑦ
ᐊᐅᑦᑕᕐᐊᐃᖅᲇᖅᲇᑦ, ᕐᐋᒍᔫᖅ ᑐᑎᐊᲇᒐᕐᐊᕐᖅᲇᖅᑐᒍ ᐅᕐᑎᑦᑕᐊᑕᕐᲇᒍ

O ne day, Kiviuq made the final decision to leave the old woman. She was beginning to scare him.

Kiviuq headed for his qajaq. Before he reached the beach, a woman's buttocks appeared and blocked his path.

The buttocks would not allow him to pass until he had sex with it. So, he mounted it. Then he was able to get away in his qajaq.

When he reached land again, he beached his qajaq and came across a big pot of boiling water.

ᐊᓂᒍᐊᓪᓚᕆᐊᕐᒪᒍ ᐃᓐᓇᖕᕆᔅᓱᓂᒎᖅ ᐅᒃᑯᓯᒃ ᑐᑎᑉᕐᑲᖅᑕᕐᒪᒍ
ᐊᓂᒍᔅᓱᐊᓚᒥᐊᖅᑐᔾᔫᒻᒪᑦ ᐊᐅᓪᓛᓕᓇᖕᔪᓂ. ᐊᒻᒪᒎᖅ
ᐊᐅᓛᕐᑲᑦᑖᓗᐊᖅᑕᖕᕆᓱᓂᓘᓐᓃᑦ ᐊᐳᖅᓯᑦᑕᐃᓐᓇᒥᐊᓕᕐᒪᑦ ᐊᒃᓴᔾᔭᐊᒎᖅ
ᑕᐃᒃᑯᐊᒃ ᐅᕆᐊᖅᑐᔾᔫᒻᒪᓂᒃ ᓯᕗᓂᐊᓂ ᐊᓂᒍᓇᐊᕐᓗᐊᕌᖕᒐᕆᙵᒎᖅ
ᓯᕗᓂᐊᓃᕐᑲᑦᑖᒥᐊᔾᔪᒻᒪᑕ ᑕᑯᔭᓗᒃᑖᖕᕆᑦ ᑮᓗᕋᐅᑦᑕᕌᖕᒐᓂᒃ
ᐲᖅᑭᑐᐊᒥᐊᖅᐸᒃᓱᑎᒃ ᐱᑦᑕᕐᒪᓂᒃ. ᐃᓯᒫᓗᓕᕐᒥ ᐊᕕᒃᑕᖅᓱᑎᒎᖅ
ᑭᖕᒍᐱᐊᖅᑐᖅᑕᖅᓱᑎᒃ ᐅᕆᐊᓱᑕᖅᑐᔫᒻᒪᓂᒃ ᐊᕕᕆᐊᕐᒥᖕᒪᓂᒎᖅ

He tried to walk around this pot, but it kept moving and blocking his path.

Kiviuq jumped up and carefully walked along the rim. He did not tip over the pot, and was able to get away.

He continued to travel. He came across two grizzly bears that were fighting.

These grizzly bears were blocking his way, and he could not pass. The bears were fighting and viciously tearing each other apart.

ᐊᑯᓂᖕᓗᒃ ᐊᖅᐸᕐᑦᑎᕿᐊᕐᐊᑐᐊᖅᓗᓂ ᐊᓂᒍᖅᑐᕐᖢᒥᖕ
ᑕᒻᒪᑎᓂᖁᕈᑎᒃ ᐊᖃᕐᕐᐊᖅ.

ᐊᒻᒪᒍᖅ ᐊᐳᖅᑭᑕᕐᒡᕐᖅ ᑭᖕᕘᕐᐊᖅ ᑐᓗᖅᑐᖆᐅᑦᑕᖅᑐᕐᖢᓂᖕ
ᑲᓯᑲᑦᑐᕐᖢᒥᖢᓂᖕ ᐅᐃᕘᓂᖅ ᐊᕐᖃᒪᒻᖅᑐᑎᖕ ᐅᖅᑐᕐᐊᑎᐊᖅᑐᕐᖢᒪᖂᖅ
ᐊᐱᑎᐊᖂᑐᐊᖅᐸᓂᖕ ᐊᑯᓂᖕᓗᒃ ᐊᓂᒍᐊᕐᑕᕿᐊᑭᐊᖅᓄᓂ. ᖃᖏᓂ Ċᓚ
ᓯᐊᓂᖅᓱᒍ ᓇᖕᑲᖅᓱᒍ ᐊᐱᑎᐊᕐᖕᓚᓂᒃ ᐊᖅᐸᕐᓄᕐᐊᑎᐊᖅᑐᕐᖢᑦ
ᐊᖂᖅᑲᕐᖕᓚᒍᒃ ᐅᖅᑲᓚᕐᑲᕐᓴᕐᓂᕐᖢᖃᐃᑦ ᐊᑯᐊᒃ Ċᖅᖕᓚ

The bears would take several steps back and charge toward each
other. When Kiviuq saw an opening, he ran across.

Kiviuq got past them, and the bears disappeared.

He then came across two cliffs that were banging against each other.

Kiviuq wanted to make an attempt to pass them. So, when the two
cliffs separated, he ran through, carrying his qajaq sideways.

Kiviuq was a fast runner, and so, as he was running, the the back of
his parka was flapping in the wind.

ᐊᖅᐸᑐᐊᒍᔾ ᑭᖕᓂᐊᓄᑦ ᖃᖕᒪᑦᑕᖅᓯᒪᐸᔮᓂᖓᖕᒪᑦ ᐊᑯᐊᒍᖅ ᑭᑉᑎᒪᒥᑦ
ᐊᑯᐊᐃᓘᖅᖕᒃᓯᖕᒻᒪᖕᒃᔾᖅ. ᑭᐸᑵᑎᐊᒥᐊᖅᒍᒍᖅ ᐊᑯᐊᒥᐊᓯᖕᒃᓯᖕᒻᒃ. ᐊᔾᐄ....
ᖄᔾᒍᖅ ᓴᓂᖕᒃᓯᖕᑎᐸᑦ ᖄᔾᐱᑎᓂᐊᖅᓘᐊᖅᒃ. ᓯᓚᑐᖅᖕ ᓄᔾᓂᖅ,
ᑭᑉᑎᓂᑐᐊᖅᓯᖕᖅᐸᑦ ᖄᔾᓂ ᓯᖅᒥᖅᒃᖕᔾᔾ ᓴᓂᖅᖕᔾ ᓇᖕᒃᓯᓂᖅᒪᔾ
ᐊᖅᐸᑎᐊᒥᖅᔾᓂ. ᑕᐃᒪᒍᖅ ᐊᐅᖕᒌᖅᑕᑕᐅᖅᓇᖕᔾᖕ ᐃᖕᒃᐊ
ᓴᓇᓯᒪᔾ ᐊᑐᖕᒃᖅᑕᐅᑎᐅᖕᑕ ᖄᓇᔾᐊᑦ ᐊᖕᓄᖕᓂᖕᒃ ᒻᒻᖅᑐᖅᑭᒪᔾ
ᐅᔾᐅᖅᑕᔥᐊᐅᓯᖕᑦ ᐊᐅᔾᐅᔾᖕᒃ. ᑕᐃᖕᒃᐊᒍᖅ ᐊᐳᖅᑭᓄᖕᓯᒻᒥᑦ

When the cliffs closed, the flap of his parka got caught and was ripped off.

Kiviuq was a wise man, and if he had not carried his qajaq sideways he would have lost it. Because he was so wise, he survived.

Kiviuq was very tired at this point, but he continued on. Next he came to a tightrope tied to two poles. Inuit used to challenge each other by doing different stunts on these tightropes, so he had to do all kinds of different moves and performances before moving on. He balanced on his

ᓴᐱᔾᔪᐊᓕᕋᓗᐊᖅᑲᓗᓂ. ᐅᐃᕙᕿᐊᖅᑕᕋᓗᐊᕐᒪᒋᑦ ᑎᐊᓐᓇᒨᖅ ᓱᓕ ᐱᓕᐊᓂᒃᑭᕗᑦ. ᑭᓯᐊᓂᒨᖅ ᐊᑐᖅᑳᓗᒋᑦ ᐆᒃᑐᕆᐊᕐᒥᒪᑦ ᐊᔪᖕᒋᑦᑐᔫᓐᓂᕋᒥᒨᖅ ᐱᖅᑯᓯᕐᓂᒃ ᖃᓄᓗᒃᑖᖅ ᑕᐃᒃᑯᐊ ᐊᑐᒐᐅᓯᕐᒪᑕ ᓲᖅᑯᖅᑲᓗᑎᒡᓗ ᓇᖕᒋᔪᕝᔪᑎᒃ ᐊᒃᑲᓅᑉ ᖄᖓᓂ. ᑎᐊᓐᓇᒨᖅ ᐱᑦᑕᕋᓘᔭᖅᑳᖅᑲᓗᓂ ᐱᖖᒍᐊᕈᓯᓗᒃᑖᖖᒎᖅ ᐱᐊᓂᒃᑲᒥᒋᑦ ᑲᑕᒃᑲᓗᓂ, ᐱᓯᒋᐊᒥᐊᕐᒪᑦ ᑕᒻᒪᑦᑕᐃᓇᕆᕝᔪᑎᒃ. ᑎᐊᓐᓇᒨᖅ ᐊᓂᒍᖅᑕᐅᔭᖅᑲᑦᑖᖅᑲᓗᓂ ᐃᓅᒐᓂᒥᐊᓚᐅᖅᑭᒪᒻᒪᑦ.

knees and stood up and walked the tightrope. He was very skillful and talented at it. He did all the different stunts and moves that Inuit athletes do, then jumped down and went on his way.

And the rope disappeared.

Kiviuq overcame all of these obstacles and survived.

ᓯᑕᒫᖕ • Part Four

ᕿᑭᖅᑕᖅ • The Island

ᐃᕿᐊᓱᑦᑎᐊᒥᐊᓚᖅᒥᒎᖅ ᐊᐅᓪᓚᖃᑦᑖᑦᑎᐊᒥᐊᕐᓂᓗᒃᑕᕋᓗᐊᕐᒪᑦ ᐊᐳᖅᑭᑦᑕᓚᓂᖕᒥᒃ ᐊᐅᓪᓛᒐᓂᒃᑕᖕᒋᒪᑦ. ᕿᑭᖅᑕᖃᕐᒪᖕᒎᖅ ᑕᓴᒪᓂ ᐅᖅᓱᐊᑦᑎᐊᒥᐊᖅᖤᓂᒎᖅ. ᕿᑭᖅᑕᔾᔪᐊᕉᖅ ᑕᐃᒻᓇ ᒪᓃᑦᑐᓗᕿᔾᔫᕝᔪᓂ ᖃᐃᖅᑐᓗᕿᔾᔫᕝᔪᓂ. ᑕᐃᑯᖕᒐᖅᖤᓂᒎᖅ ᓯᓂᑭᐊᖅᑐᒥᐊᓚᖅᒥᖕᒪᑦ ᖃᔭᓂ ᑎᒡᕙᖅᖤᒍ. ᐃᓐᓇᕐᕕᒋᓂᐊᒑᓂᒎᖅ ᓂᐊᖁᕕᓂᑦᑎᐊᒥᐊᖅᑕᖃᕐᓂᖤᓂ, ᓱᓇᑯᓘᓐᓂᑭᐊᕉᖅ ᒪᑦᕉᓐᓂᒃ ᑕᑯᑦᑕᕐᒪᑦ, ᓱᓇᐅᕙᒎᖅ ᓂᕿᖃᔪᔫᓐᓃᒃ ᐃᓄᖕᓂᒃ. ᓯᓂᓚᖂᖕᒐᑕ

At this point, he was very tired from overcoming all of the obstacles that blocked his path.

Nevertheless, he travelled on and saw an island. The water around the island was very calm. The island seemed to be flat, but really it was quite hilly.

He left his qajaq on the rocks and went to find a place to rest. Eventually he came upon several skulls.

Unbeknownst to Kiviuq, there were two ugly beings living there that fed on humans. When the people fell asleep, they would kill and eat them.

ᑐᔅᑰᑎᑲᕐᓂᖻᒪᓂᒍᖅ ᕈᓇᐅᖃᕐᒍᖅ ᐃᖅᐊᕆᖻᒍᒐᑐᖏᖅᐳᖅ.
ᖅᑲᐅᔭᕐᖃᕐᖻᓄᓂᒃ ᑕᐃᑲᑲ ᑕᐃᑯᖌᑎᕋᖃᑲᐅᕆᖅ ᕈᓂᕋᖃᑐᖻᓂᖻᒐ
ᑕᐅᑐᕐᔾᒉᕐᔾᕙᖻᒋ. ᐊᐅᒍᖅ ᐃᖅᐊᕈᖻᒐᑎᖅᒋᒍᖅ ᐃᖃᖅᐊᒐᖅᑕ,
ᕈᓂᖓᖅᑲᖅᑎᖃᖃᒍᒍᖅ ᓂᐊᖅᑴᐊᓂᐅᕝ ᐃᓂᖏᖓ ᐅᖅᑲᖅᐸᖃᑲᑰᕦᖓ,
ᓄᑖᖃᐅᒍᖅ ᓄᑕᐅᖓᑐᖻᔾᖃᓂᒐ. ᑎᐊᖃᒍᖅ ᐅᖅᑲᐅᕐᖻᐅᒋᒐ
ᐃᖃᖃᖻᒐᖻᐊᖅᒍᖓᓂ. "ᐅᕝᖃᖻᒋᓐ "ᐅᕝᖃᖻᒋᓐ ᖻᖅᑲᖻᒐᐅᑎᖻᒍᓐᕿ
ᕈᓂᕿ ᐅᖻᐊᒐᖅ ᐃᑎᕈᖻᐊᖻᒐᕙᑎᕿ." ᑎᐊᖃᒍᖅ ᑐᖻᒉᓂ ᒪᕝᒉᐊᖅᕈᒍ

Kiviuq did not know this. All that he wanted to do was rest. He was
so tired.

As he lay down to sleep, one of the skulls warned him, "Before you
fall asleep, find a flat rock and place it on your chest; otherwise, you will end
up like me."

Kiviuq listened. He then went looking for a flat rock and found one.
He went back to lie down, hiding the rock beneath his jacket against his
chest, and pretended to sleep.

ᓵᑦᑐᕋᔾᔪᐊᕐᒥᔫᖅ ᕿᓂᖅᓱᓂ ᓵᑦᑐᕋᖃᓱᕿᓐᓂᕐᒪᖔᖅ ᖄᒥᐅᑦᑎᖅᓱᓂ. ᑎᐊᓐᓇᔫᖅ ᓯᓂᒃᑭᖅᑐᖅᑐᔾᔫᓕᕐᒪᑦ ᓯᒡᒐᑉ ᓇᓛᓂᑦ ᒪᑦᑏᒃ ᐅᐊᔪᒃ ᑕᑯᕝᔪᓂᒋᒃ ᖄᔾᔭ ᓴᓂᐊᓃᕋᐅᔭᑯᓂᑦᑐᐊᕐᓂᖅᓱᑎᒃ.

ᓴᕕᖕᓂᒃ ᐸᒥᐅᖅᑲᖕᓂᕐᒪᓂᒃ ᐃᓱᐃᒃᑲᓱᒃᑐᒃ ᐅᔭᕋᒥᐊᕐᓂᒃ. ᐱᖅᑖᔫᖅ ᖃᐃᔾᔪᐊᓕᕐᒪᑦ ᑕᑯᑕᓘᔾᔭᒃᓱᒍ ᑎᑭᓕᕐᒪᑦ ᓯᓂᒃᓯᑐᒥᐊᔾᔪᐊᕐᒪᑦ ᑎᐊᓐᓇ ᖃᒻᖑᐃᓘᔭᓕᖅᓱᓂ. ᐃᒃᓯᕙᑦᓚᑎᐊᖅᓱᓂᔫᖅ ᑕᒪᐅᖓ ᓴᓂᕌᒍᑦ ᑲᐱᑎᐊᕐᕋᓗᐊᕐᒪᒍ ᐸᒥᐅᕐᒥᓄᑦ ᓵᑐᕋᔾᔪᐊᕐᓗᖔᖅ ᑐᓱᕐᒥ

After a while, he saw two beings approaching who assumed that he was asleep.

These two beings had long, sharp tails, as hard as steel. They stopped and sharpened their tails on a rock.

Kiviuq kept an eye on these beings and saw one of them coming toward him.

It stood over Kiviuq and tried to pierce him with its sharp tail. The being's tail hit the rock instead. It accidently stabbed itself, and died. The

ᐃᖕᒥᓂᒎᖅ ᑲᐱᓂᖅᑲᐅᔪᔾᔫᒪᑦ ᑐᕐᖑᓇᑯᓂᑦᑐᐊᖅᓱᓂ ᐸᒥᐅᖕᒐᒎᖅ ᐃᒃᓯᕙᓪᓚᑎᐊᕐᒪᑦ ᑰᑦᑎᓈᖕᒐᓄᑦ ᑲᑉᐳᑦᑎᔪᔾᔫᒪᑦ ᐃᓐᓇᕐᒥ ᑐᕐᑯᔫᒥᒪᑦ. ᑕᐃᒻᓇᒎᖅ ᑲᐱᓯᒋᐊᓚᐅᖅᑐᖅ ᑐᕐᑯᒻᒪᑦ ᑖᒃᑯᐊᒎᖅ ᓂᐊᕐᑯᕕᓂᒥᐊᔾᔪᐃᑦ ᐃᓅᖕᒋᑦᑐᒥᐊᔾᔪᐃᑦ ᓂᐊᕐᑯᐃᓐᓇᔾᔪᐃᑦ ᐃᒡᓚᒥᐊᖅᑐᔾᔫᓛᑦ. ᐃᒡᓚᒥᐊᖅᑐᔾᔫᓚᕐᒪᑕᒎᖅ ᐃᓱᒪᒋᖕᒋᓱᒋᖕᒎᖅ ᓯᓂᓕᒥᐊᖅᐳᖅ.

other being tried to do the same, but it also died. All the skulls started laughing, but Kiviuq was very tired, so he fell asleep laughing with them.

ᑕᓈᒪᖕᒋ • Part Five

ᐋᔭᕐᖁᒃ • The Spider

ᖃᑭ ᐅᓚᓐᖕᓂᖅᑎᕐᒃᒍᔾᖅ ᑐᑉᖕᒪᑦ ᓯᖅᓄᓪᑎᑕᐊᒐᑦᓂᖅᒧᓂ
ᖃᓇᖕᔭᒐᐊᖕᒃᒧᓂ ᐅᖅᕪᐊᖅᑐᒐᖕᓛᓗᓂᖕ ᑐᑉᖕᒪᑦ
ᓂᑕᖕᔪᖓᑭᖅᒃᑐᓂ ᐃᒐᐅᕆᐊᖁᓂ ᐃᒥᖅᒃᑭᓇᖅᑐᒍ ᐊᐅᑕᑎᖉᖅ.
ᐅᒃᕪᐊᑦ ᓇᑭᕆᐊᓂᖕ ᐃᒐᐅᕆᐊᖅᑿᓚᑐᖕᒪᑕ. ᐊᐅᒃᖃᑯᑐᐊᖑᓂᖅᑐᓂᒍᖅ
ᖃᓯᓪᑦᓇᖕᒻᖕᒃᔾᖅ ᐅᖀᒐ ᐊᐅᖃᑯᑐᒐᓂᓕᒃᒐᓇᖅᒃᒻ. ᑕᐊᒪᒍᖅ
ᐊᕐᕀᖕᕿᐊᖅ, ᑕᐃᖅᑯᐊ ᓇᓂᖔᕐᕿᐊᑦ ᐃᓄᖑᖅᕀᒪᒃᑕᐅᓂᖅᑐᓂ, ᐃᓄᖔᕐᕿᐊᔪᖅ,

K iviuq awoke at sunrise. It was very warm. The water was very calm. He had something to eat and refilled his water sack, which was made out of a bearded seal's bladder. He then continued on.

He had not travelled far when he saw smoke coming out of a cave that had been made into a qamaq (traditional sod house).

He was curious, so he climbed to the top and looked down the

ᐃᓱᖅᑐᕐᕈᔫᒪᑦ ᖃᐃᖅᑐᒥ ᐃᒡᓗᖅᑲᕐᓂᕐᒪᖖᒎᖅ ᓴᓇᐅᒐᒥᒃ ᖃᕐᒪᕋᓗᒻᒫᖅ. ᐃᓱᖅᑐᒥᐊᔾᔪᐊᖀᖅ ᑕᑯᒻᒪᒍ ᑕᑯᔭᖅᑐᐸᑦᓰᒻᒪᒍ ᐱᖅᑲᔭᓚᐅᖅᓯᒪᔮ ᑕᐃᑉᓱᒪ, ᑕᐃᑯᖕᒐᒎᖅ ᐃᒐᓕᐊᒍᑦ ᑕᑲᓄᖕᒐ ᐃᑦᓱᐊᖅᑐᓕᕐᒪᒍ ᐊᕐᓇᔾᔪᐊᖀᖅ ᐃᒐᑦᓗᓇᒃᑲᑦᑎᐊᒥᐊᖅᑐᖅ. ᓇᑭᓗᒃᑖᖀᖅ ᐱᓚᒃᑭᕙᒃᕈᓂ ᑕᑉᓗᕋᓗᖕᒥᓂᑦ, ᕿᖕᒐᕋᓗᖕᒥᓂᑦ, ᖃᑉᓗᕋᓗᖕᒥᓂᑦ, ᓯᐅᑎᕋᓗᐊᓂᑦ, ᐃᓴᕿᑕᕐᓂ ᓇᑲᑎᖅᑕᖅᕈᑎᑦ ᐃᖕᒥᓂᒎᖅ ᐆᔪᓕᐅᖅᑐᖅ. ᓱᓇᔾᔫᓐᓂᑭᐊᖅ

chimney. Inside he saw a large woman cooking. Actually, it was a spider that had turned into a human being—a being known as an Amajurjuk or Aasivak.

The woman was cutting pieces off of her chin, her nose, her eyebrows, and her ears. She put them in a pot to boil.

Kiviuq felt mischievous, so he started spitting on her head. Every

ᐊᖅᐊᒃᕐᒥᓗᓴᐊᑉᖅ ᐊᒪᕐᖅᕐᒃᐊᖅ. ᐊᒪᖅᓂᕐᐊᕐᖅᐱᐊᖕᒥᖅ ᑕᐱᑭᐊ
ᐊᒃᑐᒡᐊᕐᖅᐊᖅᓂᒪᒃᒥᑕᑊ.

ᐊᖕᒪᖕᔅᖃᐅᖅᐸᐊᖕᓐᕐᒪᒍᒡᖅ ᕐᖅᒃᒪᔅᖃᐸᖅᑐᒍ, ᓇᐊᖕᐊᒍᖅ
ᕐᖅᒃᒪᔅᖃᒪᒍ ᑕᒪᐊᖕᒪ ᓂᐊᕐᑯᐊᖂᑊ ᕐᖅᒃᒪᖅ ᑐᑕᑕᔅᖕᑊᖅ, "ᐃᒃᒃᐃᒃᐃᖅᖅ,"
ᓇᐊᖕᐊᒍᖅ ᐱᐊᒃᑕᓘᒃᑕᖅᑐᒪᐅᕐᐊᖅ. ᑕᐊᒪᒍᖅ ᕐᖅᒃᒪᒃᒪᒍ ᑭᖕᒍᑕᖅᐸᒪᖅ,
"ᐃᒃᒃᐃᒃᐃᖅᖅ, ᐅᐸᑐᒪ ᑯᕐᖅᐸᒪᓗᖕᒃᑕᑐᖅ ᑯᕐᐸᒪᓗᐳᖅᖅ." ᐊᑐᓇᐊᖅᑐᓂᒍᖅ

time the spit landed on her head she would say, "Ikkikiqiq." She would repeat this each time.

The last time that Kiviuq spat on her, she said again, "Ikkikiqiq," and looked up to see where the spit was coming from. Kiviuq hid.

The female being grabbed her ulu and cut off her eyelids. She left her

ᐅᖅᑲᑉᐱᓗᖕᒪᑦ ᑕᑯᕕᓗᒐᔭᐊᓇᒐᒥᐅᒎᖅ ᑕᓕᕆᐊᖅᑐᖅ ᑮᓈ ᐅᓗᔾᔭᐊᓂᒎᖅ ᑖᒪᓇ ᑭᐱᓯᑦᑕᕈᑎᓂ ᓇᒃᑲᖅᓱᒍ ᐊᓂᐊᓚᔅᓇᐊᖅᑐᕐᔮᒪᑦ ᓯᒡᔭᒧᖕᒎᖅ ᑭᕕᐅᖅ ᐊᖅᐸᑦᑎᐊᒥᐊᓕᖅᒪᑦ ᐊᖑᐹᒥᐊᕈᓯᖕᒐᔭᖕᒪᒍᒍᒎᖅ. ᑕᒡᕙᒎᖅ ᐃᓴᖕᒐᔮᑐᐃᓐᓇᐅᓕᖅᑎᔾᔪ ᓵᕕᐊᓪᓚᕆᐊᖅᓱᓂ ᐃᓄᖅᑭᒻᒪᒍ ᐅᖅᑲᑉᐱᓘᔭᒻᒫᓯᖕᒐᔭᓕᖅᒪᖖᒎᖅ ᐅᓗᔾᔭᐊᕐᒥᓄᖖᒎᖅ ᑕᒪᓐᓇ ᖃᐃᖅᑐᔾᔭᐊᖅ ᖃᔨᒃᑕᖅᓱᒍ, "ᓂᐊᓇᓕᓰᖅ ᓇᖕᓂᖅᑲᔅᓴᕐᔭᐃᑉᐱᑦ," ᐅᓚᒪᒃᑭᑦᑕᖅᑐᔩᒻᒪᖕᒎᖅ

tent with her ulu. Kiviuq ran away as fast as he could.

She almost caught up to Kiviuq, but he was able to get to his qajaq. She tried to force Kiviuq off the qajaq, but he got free.

The female being began pounding the ground with her ulu, cutting off large chunks of rock.

ᖃᐃᖅᑐᒥᒃ ᐅᓗᔾᔪᐊᕐᒥᓄᑦ. ᑕᐃᒪᒨᖅ ᑭᕕᐅᖅ ᐊᓐᓇᑉᖃᑦᑎᐊᒥᐊᖅᑐᖅ ᐊᕙᑕᓂᒨᖅ ᐊᓇᐅᓕᕆᐊᓐᓈᖅᖢᒧ ᐅᖃᕐᒪᑦ, “ᓂᐊᓇᓕᑉᑕᐅᓰᖅ ᓇᖕᓂᖃᑦᓚᕋᔭᐃᑉᐱᑦ.” ᑖᒻᓇ ᐊᕙᑕᔾᔪᐊᖓ ᐱᖅᐸᓗᒡᔪᐊᕐᕆᐊᖅᑐᔫᒻᒪᑦ ᐊᓇᐅᒻᒪᒧ ᖁᑭᕋᒥᐅᒨᖅ ᑐᖁᖢᓯᖕᖓᔭᖕᒪᑦ.

Kiviuq began pounding the sealskin float on his qajaq with his paddle. The noise was deafening, and the sound killed the female being.

ᐊᐃᑕᕐᑭᑐᖅ • Tʜᴇ Wᴀʏ Hᴏᴍᴇ

ᑕᐃᒪ ᐱᐊᓂᖕᒪᖖᒎᖅ ᑕᐃᒻᓇ ᐱᔭᐅᖃᔭᕐᓂᑯᐊ ᖃᓂᓐᓈᓕᕐᓂᕐᒪᑕ. ᐊᐅᓪᓚᓵᑐᐃᓐᓇᐅᓚᕐᒥ ᐃᓄᒃᓱᓈᒎᖅ ᑕᐃᒃᑯᐊ ᒪᑦᕿᐱᔾᔪᐊᒃ ᑕᒃᐹᓂ ᕿᑭᖅᑕᑉ ᖄᖓᓂ ᑐᖅᓲᒥᐊᓱᑦᑐᐊᓕᕐᒥᒪᓂᒃ ᑑᓵᓐᓇᓚᐅᕋᓱᐊᖅᓱᑎᒃ. “ᐅᕐᕕᖅᓱᕿᐅᑉ ᑎᒍᓇᕚᑎᕐ! , ᐅᕐᕕᖅᓱᕿᐅᑉ ᑎᒍᓇᕚᑎᕐ!” ᐅᑯᒥᐊᖅᑕᐱᑐᐃᓐᓇᐅᒻᒪᓂᒎᖅ ᐃᓄᒃᑯᓐᓈᒃ ᐃᓅᖕᒋᑦᑐᒃ ᐅᑯᔾᔪᒃᑕᖅᑐᖅ. ᑐᖅᓵᓗᐊᒧᑦ “ᑎᒍᓇᕚ…!!”. ᑎᐊᓇᐃᓕᐅᓗᐊᓕᕐᒪᓂᒎᖅ

After overcoming this obstacle, Kiviuq continued his journey and came across two small inuksuit on top of a hill.

The inuksuit were yelling at Kiviuq. At first he tried to ignore them. They were yelling, “Clams might grab you, clams might grab you.” Although they were not human, they were bending down and yelling to him.

Kiviuq tried to ignore them, but eventually he no longer could, so he

ᑖᕗᖓᒎᖅ ᑭᖑᒻᒧᑦ ᕿᕕᐊᕐᔫᒥᒻᒪᑦ ᐸᖁᒥᓱᖏᑦᑎᐊᒥᐊᕋᓗᐊᕋᒥ.
ᑖᑯᐊᒎᖅ ᐅᕐᕕᖅᖢᕐᔪᐊᔾᔪᐊᒃ ᐊᖏᔪᖢᔾᔪᐊᒃ ᖄᔭᑕ ᑭᖑᓂᐊᓂ
ᑮᓯᑉᐹᑦᑎᐊᒥᐊᖅᑕᓕᖅᑑᓐᓃᒃ ᖄᕕᐊᖅᒪᒋᒃ ᐊᖅᑲᓇᐊᑯᓗᒻᒫᖅᖢᑎᒎᖅ
ᐅᖅᑲᓱᖕᒐᔭᖕᒪᓂᒃ, "ᑕᒃᐱᑯᐊᓕ ᖁᐸᓗᖅᓱᖅ, ᓴᐸᓗᓱᖅ ᖃᐸᓗᖅ."
ᓴᓪᓗᓂᖃᐃᔾᔪᑎᒎᖅ ᑭᕕᓱᖕᒐᔭᖕᒪᓂᒃ.

ᑎᑭᓴᖅᑐᓕᖅᒪᖖᒎᖅ ᐊᑖᑖᓗᒎᖅ ᐊᓈᓈᓗ

looked behind and saw two giant clams. They were very close to grabbing the back of Kiviuq's qajaq.

Then they submerged again, taunting him as they submerged into the water.

If he had not turned to look, his qajaq would have been destroyed. Kiviuq had travelled for a long time, and through very rough circumstances, but finally he started recognizing the landscape. He knew this place.

ᓂᕆᐅᕐᑲᑦᑖᑦᑎᐊᒥᐊᕐᓂᕐᒪᓂᒃ ᐊᐅᔾᖑᕐᑲᓕᕐᒪᑦ ᐊᐃᖏᑕᐃᓐᓇᕐᓂᕐᒪᓂᒨᖅ ᑕᐃᒪᖕᖓᓂᒍᒃᑖᖅ ᓵᕕᑕᐅᒻᒪᑦ. ᑐᐱᖕᖑᖕᒨᖅ ᐊᐃᖏᑕᐃᓐᓇᕐᓂᕐᒪᓂᒃ ᑭᕕᐅᕐᒥᒃ ᐅᑕᖅᑭᔪᒥᐊᔾᔪᐃᑦ. ᑕᐃᒪᒨᖅ ᐃᕆᐊᓪᓚᒃᑕᓕᕐᒪᑦ ᓄᓇᓂ ᐃᓕᑕᕆᔾᔪᐊᕆᓪᒪᒍ ᐅᕙᒍᐃ ᑕᐃᑲᓃᓐᓂᖅᐸᑕ ᐃᕆᐊᓪᓚᒃᑕᓕᕐᒪᑦ ᑕᐃᒪᒨᖅ ᐊᖕᒐᔪᖅᑳᕆᒃ ᑕᒪᕐᒥᒃ ᑎᐊᓐᓇᒨᖅ ᐅᕐᑲᖅᑕᐅᔭᓕᖅᑐᒃ, ᐄ... ᐄ.... ᓲᕐᓗ ᑭᕕᐅᑉ ᓂᐹ, ᑎᐊᓐᓇᐃᓕᐅᓕᕐᒪᓂᒨᖅ ᓯᓇᐅᕙᒨᖅ ᑭᕕᐅᔾᔪᐊᖅ

The people from his old camp were on the shore waiting for him, yelling at him, excited to see him.

Kiviuq recognized his home and began yelling, out of joy, expecting to see his parents.

His mother recognized his voice and said, “Is that Kiviuq’s voice I hear?” And it was Kiviuq!

Both his parents had been waiting patiently for his return, and they

ᐃᓂᐊᑦᒥ ᑲᒐᑦᑐᒪᓂᖕ ᐅᔭᖕᕆᒥᕐᑐᖕ.

ᑕᒪᓗᖕᖑ ᑭᐱᐅᖕ ᓂᑦᑐᕐᔪᓪᒪᕐ ᓯᓕᔪᐊᕈᑎᕆᐅᒪᒪᓂᖕ
ᖃᑯᐊᑦᑦᓐᔫᔪᐊᖑᕐ ᖃᑯᐊᑦᑦᑕᓐᖕᒪᕐ ᐃᓇᖕᒪ ᑐᖕᑯᐊᖅᖑᔪᕐᒪᕐ.
ᖃᑯᐊᑦᑦᓐᔫᔪᐊᒥᖕᖕᒥᖕ ᐃᓐᑕᓐᔫᑐᐊᖕᒍ ᖃᑯᐊᑦᑕᓐᔫᕐ
ᑐᖕᑯᕐᒪᕐᔪᓪᒪᓂᖕ ᐊᖕᓚᖕᖕᒃᖕᕆᑎᑕᐅᖕᔪᖕ. ᐊᒪᒍᖕᖕ ᒪᕐᖒᓂᖕ
ᓅᑕᖕᑲᐅᑦᖕᓂᕐᒪᕐ ᐱᖕᑲᒍᖕᖕ ᐱᖑᓂᖕᖅᖕᑲᐅᑕᐅᕐᔪᐊᖕᒍ ᐱᖕᑲᕐ

ᕿᓐᑎᒍᐊᖕᕆᓂᖅᑲ ᐅᐸᕈ. ᑕᐃᓚ ᖕᒥ ᕿᓐᑎᓂᖅᑲᐅᑉ ᐊᔾᔨᒻ
ᐅᐃᐸᕝᓂᓪᒃ ᐴᓚ ᒥ ᕿᓐᑎᕝᖕᕆᓂᖅᑲᐅᒐᐅ ᑭᕿᐅᔭᖖᒥ
ᑭᕕᖕᔪᑎᓂᔾᐊᕝᕆ ᖏᐸᑎᓂᔾᐊᕝᕆ ᒪᓇᐅᒻ ᓄᖕᓄᓂᖕᒃ ᐸᓂᔭᐃᓂᖕᒃ
ᕿᓐᑎᓂᖅᑲᐅᑕᖕᒥᔾᒻ ᑕᐃᓇ ᕿᓐᑎᓂᖅᑲᐅᑕᐅᖏᔪᐊᓄ
ᐱᓯᐊᖕᕆᒡᑕᐅ.

    When Kiviuq saw this, he grew to love her more than his other wife.
Kiviuq did not want the wife who had remarried back. He lived with the
woman who had been faithful.

ᑕᖕᐊ ᐃᕆᐊ
The End

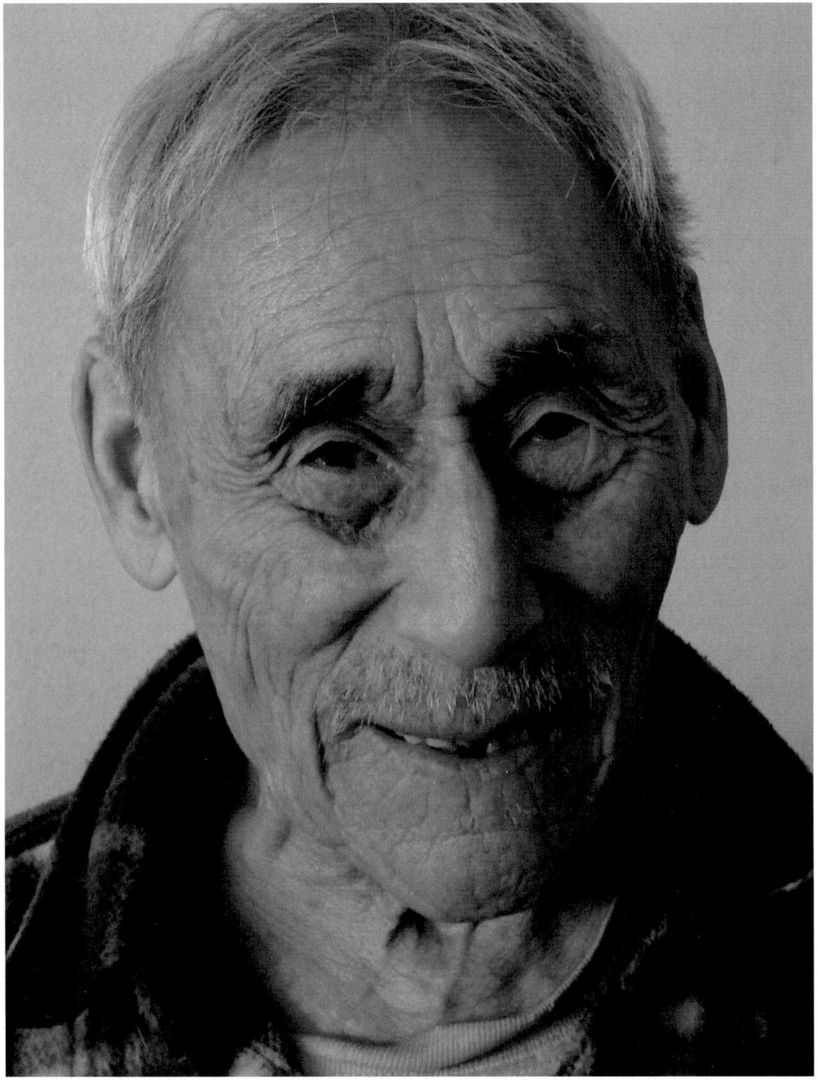

ᕼᐃᓐᓂ ᐃᖢᐊᕐᓂᖅ ᐃᓅᓚᐅᖅᑐᖅ
ᐊᕐᕕᐊᒥ (1925-2012)
ᐃᓐᓇᐅᓚᐅᖅᑐᖅ ᐅᓂᑉᑳᖅᑎᐊᓪᓗᓂ
ᐊᕐᕕᐊᓂ ᓄᓇᕘᒥ.
ᐃᖢᐊᕐᓂᖅ ᖃᐅᔨᒪᔭᐅᑦᑎᐊᖅᑐᖅ
ᐃᖅᑲᐅᒪᑦᑎᐊᕋᓂᖓᓄᑦ
ᐊᑕᖐᑦᑎᐊᖅᖢᓂ
ᐅᓂᑉᑳᖅᑐᐊᕐᓂᒃ ᐱᓯᕐᓂᒡᓗ
ᐊᒻᒪ ᐊᒥᖅᑳᕐᑲᑎᕐᑲᕈᒪᓂᖓ
ᕐᑲᐅᔨᒪᓂᕐᒥᓂᒃ ᐃᓄᖕᓄᑦ.
ᐃᖢᐊᕐᓂᕐᓗ ᓄᑲᖅᑖᖓᓗ
ᒫᑯᓯ ᑐᓂᓯᕐᔪᐊᖅᓯᒪᔪᒃ
ᐊᓐᓇᒃᑐᐃᓯᒪᑉᓗᑎᒡᓗ
ᐱᒻᒪᕆᐅᑎᑦᑎᑉᓗᑎᒃ ᐃᓄᐃᑦ
ᐅᓂᑉᑳᖅᑐᐊᑐᕐᑲᖏᓐᓂᒃ.

Henry Isluanik (1925-2012) was an elder and storyteller from Arviat, Nunavut. Henry was well known for his memory of stories and songs, and for his generosity in sharing his knowledge with people. Henry and his brother, Mark Kalluak, contributed greatly to the preservation and promotion of Inuit traditional stories.